Betty Sweet
Tells All

ALSO BY JUDITH MINTHORN STACY
Maggie Sweet

Betty Sweet Tells All

JUDITH MINTHORN STACY

HarperCollins*Publishers*

This is a work of fiction. The characters, incidents, and dialogues are products of the author's imagination and are not to be construed as real. Any resemblance to actual persons, living or dead, is entirely coincidental.

HarperCollins books may be purchased for educational, business, or sales promotional use. For information, please write: Special Markets Department, HarperCollins Publishers Inc., 10 East 53rd Street, New York, NY 10022.

FIRST EDITION

Designed by Jackie McKee

Library of Congress Cataloging-in-Publication Data

Stacy, Judith Minthorn.
Betty Sweet Tells All/ Judith Minthorn Stacy.—1st ed.
p. cm.
ISBN 0-06-018485-X
1. Southern States—Fiction. 2. Mothers and daughters—Fiction. 3. Beauty operators—Fiction. 4. Divorce—Fiction. I. Title.

PS 3569.T145 V5 2002
813'.54—dc21
20011024863

02 03 04 05 06 ❖/RRD 10 9 8 7 6 5 4 3 2 1

To Ben, Roger, Linda, Michael, Christopher,
and their families, with love

Acknowledgments

....

I WOULD LIKE TO THANK my parents, Robert and Ethel Minthorn, who passed their love of reading on to me.

My stepmother, Mary, whose enthusiasm for my writing continues to delight and surprise me.

I thank my sisters Joanne, Margaret, Nancy, and Susan for their unfailing support and friendship.

I am deeply grateful to my writers' group: Maggie Allen, Jean Beatty, Ann Campanella, Jeanne Faulconer, Ruth Ann Grissom, Lisa Kline, Nancy Lammers, and Carolyn Noell, whose encouragement has been invaluable to me.

Finally, thanks to Carolyn Marino and Erica Johanson, who made publishing this book a reality.

Betty Sweet
Tells All

JUNE 1985

1

Betty

....

June 5, 1985

Dear Annie,

I'm sorry it's taken me so long to answer your letter, but the worst thing in the world has happened.

Maggie has gone and left Steven! Nineteen years of marriage and she just up and left him the day after their girls graduated from high school. The whole town's talking and I'm just sick about it. I never in all my life thought she'd do such a thing. I mean, she's my daughter and I love her, but I don't understand what she's thinking.

I don't know what's going to happen next—what Maggie thinks life is all about. She's thirty-eight years old, but sometimes I think she had better sense in her twenties. It's probably one of those midlife crisis things all the magazines write about, but when the dust settles and she gets back to her old self, she's going to regret this for the rest of her life.

I always thought I knew Maggie, knew her to the core. Now, I wonder if anyone ever knows anyone else. I mean, to leave a perfectly good husband for a job at the Curl & Swirl and that dinky little apartment behind the shop! It just doesn't make sense.

But when I try to talk to her about it, all she'll say is, "You don't know, Mother. You just don't know."

Well, she's right about that! I sure as the world don't know. But I'd like to jerk a knot in her tail.

I'm sorry this is such a depressing letter. But I wanted you to know why I haven't written and why I won't be coming for a visit like I promised.

Mama Dean's about to go crazy and about to drive me crazy, too. I know she's just as sick about this whole thing as I am, but it'd be a whole lot easier if she wouldn't let me know morning, noon, and night 'I told you so.'

You've been like a sister to me since high school. I just wish you didn't live so far away. You're the only one I can confide in and I need someone to talk sense to me. Tell me what to do to stop all this mess before Maggie ruins her life forever. It seems like I'm supposed to do something, but when I think about it my mind goes round and round in circles and I get slicing pains in my chest.

Please write back soon. I need a friend!

Love,
Betty

Dear Betty,

I am shocked in my heart! I always thought Maggie had this perfect life! Every time my kids did something crazy, I'd always think about Maggie never giving anyone a bit of trouble.

You asked me what I thought Maggie wanted, what she thought life was about? The truth is, I don't know. I don't know what anyone is thinking—what anyone expects out of life. Used to, I thought I did. But the older I get the less I seem to know.

I do know about small-town gossip though—what everyone must be saying about Maggie leaving a perfectly good husband.

(Though, I've yet to meet a PERFECTLY good husband! Ha Ha!)

I know blood is thicker than water and you want to be there when she is ready to talk. But there isn't much you can do until then. She's old enough to live her own life and pay the consequences if she's made a mistake. Worrying yourself to death won't change a thing.

Maybe it's easy for me to say, since Maggie isn't my daughter, but you sound so torn up. Your job, Mama Dean, and now Maggie! As Matt Dillon said on Gunsmoke, *"It's time to get out of Dodge."*

Wait 'til you see my new double-wide! There's a great room with a fireplace, a huge country kitchen with built-in everything, two bedrooms, each with its own bathroom and garden-tub, all done up in mauves and blues. Say you'll come and you can have the "mauve suite" for as long as you want.

We could walk on the beach, feed the sea gulls, and talk. I can't wait for you to meet my friends in the Brunch Bunch.

It's hard to believe I've lived here at Ocean Isle for three years now— even harder to believe it's been that long since my Ed passed away.

The other day, I heard K. T. Oslin's song "80's Ladies." It reminded me of how we used to be. Especially the part about, one was pretty, one was smart, the other was a borderline fool. Well, you were the one who was pretty and smart. I'm still the borderline fool.

Remember when we used to sneak cigarettes, play Patsy Cline records, and talk all night?

I know you Capricorns are practical and long-suffering. But promise you won't be an old Capricorn about this. You need a vacation. There's more to life than work, worry, and wondering what the neighbors might say. Knowing you, you've probably got a couple of hundred vacation days coming, so I won't take no for an answer.

Love,

Annie

. . .

"I never thought I'd say such a thing about my own granddaughter," Mama Dean says, as she wads up her church bulletin and stuffs it into her purse. "But Maggie Sweet always did admire wildness. She takes after her daddy that way."

Betty pulls the car into the driveway and parks. Preacher Poteat's sermon seemed to go on forever this morning and she already has a headache. "Lord, Mama. She isn't the least bit like Smiling Jack. I don't know much, but there's one thing I do know. Maggie's always been deep, and life's extra hard on the deep ones. Why, I've seen her staring out the window up the road for years. I just never thought . . ."

Betty gets out of the car and walks around it to help Mama Dean out of the passenger's side, but when she reaches for her mother's arm, Mama Dean glares and jerks away. "Well, she sure as the world doesn't take after our side of the family," she says.

As they start up the porch steps, Betty says absently, "I know she's young, but maybe she's going through the change of life—an early change."

"She's going through the change all right. I think she's gone and lost her simple mind."

Betty unlocks the front door and sighs again. They'd been having this same conversation for weeks.

Mama Dean lowers herself slowly into a chair by the window. "Am I a bad person? Tell me if you think I've been a bad person. I don't know what I've ever done to deserve all this."

Betty sets her purse on the coffee table and goes to the window to open the curtains. "Don't start, Mama. Please don't start."

Mama Dean ignores her. "Law, me. Now I have to turn my head

every time I go uptown. Why, at church this morning, Gladys Spivey flat out said, 'Isn't it a shame your granddaughter has gone and ruined her life.'"

"Gladys Spivey thinks she's on a first-name basis with God! If she's going to be so holier-than-thou, I think you all need to drop her from your Friday night poker club," Betty says.

"She said it right to my face! Right there in the vestibule in front of God and Preacher Poteat. I tell you, I just stood there. I didn't know what to say." Mama Dean purses her lips, then groans as she bends to unhook her stockings, which she rolls down around her ankles like deflated balloons.

Betty sighs again. Even if Mama Dean hadn't known what to say, the look she'd given Gladys Spivey should have frozen the old woman into silence forever. Betty knows Mama Dean's looks. She's been at the mercy of those looks her whole life.

It's noon, Sunday. Betty has the whole day off from work. A whole day to spend with Mama Dean, who suddenly has plenty to say and will probably spend the entire day saying it. Betty kicks off her pumps and goes out to the kitchen to start Sunday supper—pot roast, potatoes, and baby carrots she'll have simmering in the Crock-Pot before lunch.

Mama Dean's voice follows her. "I tell you, the young people in this town is going downhill in a handbasket. I just never thought I'd live to see the women getting as selfish and no-account as the men. Why, Maggie Sweet had everything a body could want—a family, a fine home in the historical part of town, that add-a-pearl necklace . . ."

There was no doubt about it. Maggie Sweet was wrong to do what she'd done, but Betty can't stand to hear anyone criticize her. Maggie is her daughter, her own little girl. It's all right for her to criticize her daughter, but it flies all over her when someone else does. Even if that someone is Mama Dean.

"I can't tell you how excited I am to be hearing about this for the millionth time this week," Betty mutters, as she rummages through the cupboard for the Crock-Pot. She finds it, washes her hands, the Crock-Pot, and the potatoes.

Mama Dean's voice drifts out to the kitchen. "I tell you, I did everything I knew to do and then some. I just don't know where we went wrong."

Betty turns the water on full force and peels the potatoes and carrots, then she puts the roast in the Crock-Pot, adds the vegetables, and covers everything with Lipton's Onion Soup mix.

When she turns off the water, she can hear Mama Dean's voice again. She turns the radio on low. A country-oldies station is playing "Little Rosewood Casket." Betty sighs. She'd rather have her last tooth drilled than to hear that depressing song. She flips the dial until it lands on Emmylou Harris singing "One of These Days."

She stares out the kitchen window. Mama Dean is still talking, but Betty can't make out the words anymore. She turns up the volume. Now all she can hear is Emmylou. She rummages under the sink again, behind the trash bags and Comet and Ivory liquid, until her fingers touch a dusty bottle. There it is! The homemade dandelion wine Dr. Pinckney's nurse had given her at the hospital Christmas party. Betty isn't sure why she's kept it all these months, but somehow just knowing it's there makes her feel she still has a private life, one thing in her life that no one would ever suspect. Why, everyone in town knows the only alcohol Mama Dean allows in the house is Eckerd's rubbing alcohol.

Betty opens the bottle, pours a half inch into a Flintstone juice glass, and carries it out to the backyard.

She barely notices the bright Carolina blue sky or the sweet heavy scent of honeysuckle. All she sees is the paint peeling off the house, the grass that needs mowing, and the garden that's gone to weed. She'd like nothing better than to mow it all down, but the ancient lawn mower is about to breathe its last.

Betty feels defeated. There is more to do than she can say grace over. They should put the old place up for sale, move into one of the new condominiums that are springing up all over town with their central air-conditioning, dishwashers, and smooth green lawns. But Mama Dean won't hear of it, won't even discuss it.

Betty shakes her head and wonders why she even bothers with a garden anymore. The pantry shelves already sag with canning jars from past seasons—enough food to feed all the neighbors within a two-block radius.

With Maggie's daughters about to go off to college, they'll have to hire a schoolboy to help around the place. But schoolboys don't mow yards these days. Instead, they bully their parents into buying them cars and Nintendo or hang out at the mall scaring senior citizens.

Lord, she was acting as old and cross as Mama Dean—starting her sentences with "back in my day" or "young people nowadays." A sure sign of impending old age. But she does feel old and the world does seem to be going to hell in a handbasket.

What she really wants is to rent a haymower or a backhoe and level everything in sight.

Betty turns her back on the peeling paint, the garden gone to weed, the unmowed grass, and imagines the *Expositor* headline.

POPLAR GROVE WOMAN RUNS
AMOK WITH BACKHOE

Betty Sweet, 102 Magnolia Street, has been charged with reckless operation and abandonment of a motor vehicle. In a statement to police, Ms. Sweet said, "I could have sworn I hit the brakes, but I must have hit the gas pedal instead. Next thing I knew the place was leveled, house and all. I guess I was lucky to have been thrown clear because that old backhoe just kept going 'til it run plumb out of gas."

Mrs. Deanie Pruitt, Ms. Sweet's mother and owner of the property, could not be reached for comment.

Neighbors and co-workers stated that Ms. Sweet had seemed depressed recently.

An unidentified source said, "She always stayed pretty much to herself. I guess you'd have to call her a loner."

Although uninjured, Ms. Sweet, who refused to give her age, was shaken and confused. Her only concern was the whereabouts of a Flintstone juice glass.

Betty grins, stretches out on a chaise lounge, and sips the sweet, caustic wine. Lord, Lord, she has come to a sorry place—drinking dandelion wine at high noon in her church dress, and daydreaming about vandalism.

2

Betty

"Leaving a husband seems to run in the family." That's what Maggie had said. Betty sits up in bed as the words hit her. Now she tries to gather her thoughts as they float above her in the dark, refusing to be collected.

It's 4 A.M., June. The hottest June on record. Betty is fifty-six. Mama Dean, seventy-four, is sleeping like a rock in the next room. Betty hears her mother snore, roll over, and mutter, "Lordhavemercy."

Even in her sleep, Mama Dean is toting up people's sins.

Betty used to be clear about sin. Now she wonders.

To all outward appearances, they are a satisfied pair. Mother and daughter, living out their years in Mama Dean's old boardinghouse. They've lived together since Betty disgraced the family thirty-four years before by divorcing her husband and bringing her four-year-old daughter, Maggie Sweet, home to live in Poplar Grove.

Until recently Betty had been satisfied with this arrangement, or if not completely satisfied, at least her life had seemed neat and orderly.

Now she wonders what ever happened to that neat, orderly life or if she'd just fooled herself into believing that life could ever be neat and orderly.

Betty's always been practical. Even her job is practical. She's a Licensed Practical Nurse and has worked the swing shift at Providence Hospital for more than thirty years.

Last year the hospital had been sold. It was now called the Poplar Grove Long Term Care Facility. Betty works swing shift in the Alzheimer Unit. Everyone says she's cool, calm, and collected. A rock in a crisis. She's always taken pride in people seeing her that way. But now she is filled with confusion and something that feels like longing, even though she doesn't know what it is that she's longing for.

This is new territory. Until recently she'd refused to *believe* in confusion and longings. Now, those pushed-down feelings have taken over her life, popping out at the oddest moments. Two thousand pounds of confusion and longings stuffed into a hundred and fifteen pound woman.

She gets quietly out of bed and remembers the bottle of dandelion wine under the sink. But thinking about dandelion wine at 4 A.M. scares her and she climbs back into the wide, empty bed.

She'd probably be better off taking up Valium or smoking. This afternoon she'll buy some Stress-Tabs, ask Dr. Pinckney to check her hormone levels.

She has an impulse to call Maggie. But it's too early. Maggie would rush to the phone in a panic, breathless, wondering who'd died. Besides, *he* might answer. Betty isn't ready for that.

She looks at the clock again. In forty-five minutes it will be time to get ready for work. She gets up and goes to the kitchen to start the coffee. While it's brewing she thinks about Annie's letters. For years those letters have been a lifeline. They've seen each other through everything—marriage, birth, divorce, and death. Good times and bad. But in spite of all that, Betty has put off writing *the* letter. The letter that will tell Annie what's really going on.

When the coffee is ready, she pours out a mug, tears a sheet of paper from a tablet by the phone, and settles in at the kitchen table to write.

Dear Annie,

Thanks for the beach offer. But with all that's going on here, I just can't get away right now. (What do you mean, "don't be an old Capricorn"? I know there's more to life than work, worry, and wondering about the neighbors. But sometimes life's just hard. Besides, I don't believe in any of that horoscope stuff anyway—they've never been able to prove any of it.)

Mama Dean's still driving me crazy. But I'd feel too guilty leaving her on her own right now. And I'm still worried to death about Maggie.

Did I tell you that when she left Steven she told Mama Dean and me that leaving a husband seems to run in the family! I cannot tell you how much that hurt me. I did leave a husband, but that was thirty-four years ago. She made it sound like I go through husbands like Mama Dean goes through Sweet 'N Low.

At first I thought she said it to hurt me. Now I think she said it to make herself feel better. But her leaving Steven isn't anything like me leaving Jack. Steven never was one to drink. Besides, they'd been married nineteen years. How bad could it be if they'd been together that long? Couldn't they have worked it out? They're both good people. I always thought two good people could work anything out.

But it seems that everything I thought about life turns out to be wrong.

Annie, I've got something to tell you—something I haven't told to another soul. I've known this for weeks, but was too ashamed to tell anyone—even you. I think Maggie has taken up with her old high school sweetheart. A while back, I saw a pickup with Florida license plates parked behind her apartment and suddenly everything just came together and I knew.

The old boyfriend's name is Jerry Roberts. Maggie dated him all through high school and was crazy about him. (Do you remember when we sent her off to live with her daddy the minute she graduated? Jerry Roberts is why we did it. After what I went through at her age, I just couldn't take the chance of history repeating itself.)

Anyway, this past spring he came up here from Florida for their twentieth class reunion and before you could say Jack Robinson, he'd bought his old family homeplace and decided to stay.

Well, the minute I saw that truck, something in my mind just clicked. I mean, for her to leave Steven after all those years just when her old boyfriend turns up!

I cannot tell you how I felt. I don't know if you'll understand this. I don't even understand it myself. But when I saw that truck, I did the oddest thing. I drove off like I'd done something wrong. Like I'd read someone's diary and knew something I wasn't supposed to know. Something I'd give anything not to know.

I still haven't said anything to Maggie. I wouldn't even know how to bring it up. Also, I keep hoping against hope that I'm wrong.

If it's true I want to shake her. Ask her how this could happen—

how she could let it happen. I tried so hard to raise her right. How could she do this? How could she go back on her raising?

But then I think of all the times I saw her staring out the window up the road. I knew something was wrong. I knew she wasn't happy. But I pretended not to notice. Now I wonder if I just didn't want to know.

It's the saddest thing to drive past Maggie's house and to know she's gone. Steven's still there. The girls are still there. But Maggie is gone. Used to, I drove past that house every day on my way to work. Now I try to remember to take a different route.

Don't tempt me with any more beach offers. Right now I feel like running away and never coming back. But running away never solves anything, does it? I mean, everywhere you go, there you are.

There's a sign on the hospital bulletin board that says, "When you get to the end of your rope, tie a knot in it and hold on."

Love,

Betty

P.S. Please keep those cards and letters coming. When things settle down, I really do plan to get out of Dodge.

P.S. #2 Thanks for the snapshot of the Brunch Bunch. I didn't know there were men in the group! When did you dye your hair red and get your ears pierced? It looks good. I just wasn't expecting it.

P.S. #3 Tear up this letter as soon as you've read it. If it falls into the wrong hands they'll run Maggie out of town and put me in the hospital's quiet room.

P.S. #4 Do you really think I'm a typical Capricorn?

3

Maggie

They have just pulled onto I-40 outside of Asheville when a hawk swoops low over the pickup. Jerry points skyward as it hovers over the windshield then glides off into the distance and disappears into the mountains. "Did you see that, Maggie?"

"Wow! For a second there I thought it was going to crash into us," she says.

"I've never seen a hawk so close. You could almost count its feathers, reach out and touch it," he says.

Maggie slides across the truck seat, as close to Jerry as her seat belt allows. He has short dark hair just beginning to gray at the temples and he's so long and lean that when they sit like this her head rests somewhere between his chest and shoulder. But his eyes are his best feature. Some days they're a deep cobalt blue. Other days they're as turquoise as the sea. It was true what they said about eyes being the windows to the soul. Twenty years ago, at a high school sockhop, Maggie got lost in those eyes. They still have the power to dazzle her.

Maggie gazes out the pickup window. The mountains seem

brushstroked with watercolors so pale and muted it's impossible to tell where one leaves off and the other begins.

"This weekend was great," she says. "The minute we got out of Poplar Grove, I felt like a huge weight had been lifted off me."

"Me too. Asheville's only two hours away, but it's a whole different world. We need to get away more often," he says, putting his hand on her knee.

"I loved that vintage clothing store we went to."

"That outfit you bought was great. What did you call it?"

"It's a garden-party dress from the forties. I love it. Do you think that big hat is overdoing it?"

"No way. You looked beautiful in that hat."

Maggie grins. Over the years some people have called her cute. But Jerry actually believes she's beautiful. "Thanks. But I'm not exactly the garden-party type."

"I can't wait for you to wear it," he says.

"Oh, Lord, now I'm starting to feel superstitious, like I jinxed something by buying my wedding dress so soon."

"You didn't jinx anything," he says. "It's going to happen."

"I just couldn't help myself. I want our wedding outdoors, in a garden. I want to wear my garden-party outfit, carry fresh flowers from Mother's garden, and have Daddy give me away."

They are leaving the mountains, coming into the foothills. She rolls down her window, a blast of hot air hits her, and she rolls it up again. A moment later a sign announces Poplar Grove, 36 miles.

"Oh, no! We're almost home. I wish we could just go away until everything blows over," she says.

"We knew it would be a mess for a while. We just have to hold our heads up. Go on about our business and wait it out."

"But Steven hasn't even signed the papers yet. Even if he doesn't countersue, it'll take a year for the divorce to be final."

"He won't countersue. You haven't asked for a thing but your freedom. He just got his pride hurt."

Maggie nods. "You've got that right. Steven's always been real big on pride."

Maggie's daughters float into her mind. Amy's blond shoulder-length bob, cultured pearls, and preppy clothes. Jill with a fat braid, dressing like Pocahontas. Except for being twins, the only thing her daughters have in common is a deep and abiding wish to put Poplar Grove as far behind them as possible.

"The girls go off to college in a few weeks," she says. "I hate they're leaving with such hard feelings."

"You expected that, didn't you?" he asks.

"Expecting it's a lot different than living through it. Sometimes when I call, I can hear them telling Steven to say they're not at home. I was hoping they'd let me take them school shopping or out to lunch before they leave, but if they won't even talk to me on the phone . . ." She tries to go on, but her lips tremble.

"They're upset right now, honey. Just give them time," he says, curling his long fingers around hers.

"I can't believe everyone's so surprised. Steven and I hadn't gotten along in years. The girls knew that better than anyone."

"They just never thought you'd do anything about it," he says, squeezing her hand. "You made waves. Big waves. Teenagers don't like that. They want their parents, especially their mothers, to stay quietly in the background . . . be background for their lives."

"I wish I hadn't left the way I did. I wanted to be completely grown-up about it—tell Steven first, then we'd tell the girls together. But before I could tell him we got into it about something else. He kept shouting at me—wouldn't let me defend myself. Next thing I knew I'd stomped out of the house and checked myself into the Yadkin Motel."

Jerry frowns. The traffic ahead has become heavier. Then a car speeds off an exit ramp, pulls out directly in front of them, slams on its brakes, and slows to twenty miles under the speed limit. The car, an old station wagon, has a bumper sticker that says: I DON'T SUFFER FROM INSANITY, I ENJOY EVERY MINUTE OF IT.

Maggie hadn't been at the Yadkin for five minutes before some busybody told Steven where she was. The next thing she knew he was knocking on her door, then he grabbed her and started hauling her through the motel parking lot toward his car.

She'd never been the type to make a scene in public and Steven knew it. But the minute she got one arm free, she grabbed his good Cross pen and pencil set from his shirt pocket, threw them on the ground, and stomped on them.

It was the only thing she could think to do.

For a moment they just stood there, staring at the dented pen and pencil set on the parking lot blacktop. Then, the traffic light in front of the motel turned red—cars stopped—drivers gawked.

Suddenly something in her mind clicked.

"Steven," she said. "Those people are watching. They probably think you're trying to kidnap me or something."

And Steven got in his car and peeled out of the parking lot.

Maggie smiles at the memory. It was the first time in all their years together that she'd ever won an argument with Steven.

Traffic thins out and Jerry passes the station wagon at last. She squeezes his hand and for a while they drive on in silence.

Finally, she says, "I guess I can't blame the girls for being upset. Even at my age, I can't imagine my mother making waves—that she ever made a single wave in her life. I've always thought of her as just my mother, you know?"

"How long has she lived at the boardinghouse with your Mama Dean?" he asks.

"Since I was four. Lord! That means she was only twenty-two when she divorced Daddy. I can't believe it! In all those years I don't think she ever had a date."

"Maybe she did. Maybe she had this whole secret life you never knew about."

"Jerry!"

"Would that be so bad?"

"It's just not possible."

"Well, it *is* possible, but I guess it's not likely. I hope she did, though. It'd be kind of sad if she didn't."

"For goodness' sake, Jerry! This is my mother you're talking about."

"Do you think she's guessed about us?"

"I don't think so. At first I planned to tell her, tell everyone flat out. But she hasn't been able to wrap her mind around the idea that I've actually gone and left. I think she needs a while to get used to that first."

Maggie takes a deep breath. More than anything she wants everyone to be all right. But deep down inside, she wonders if Mother and Mama Dean will ever accept Jerry, ever get used to the idea that she's left Steven. Even when she'd been a timid little girl, then a quiet, obedient housewife, Mama Dean was always expecting the worst from her. "You mark my words," she'd say. "That Maggie Sweet bears watching." And Mother would say, "Now, Mama Dean, there's no call for that. Maggie's always done the right thing and I know she'll do the right thing now."

When Maggie thinks about Mother and Mama Dean, her stomach clenches and her eyes well up.

The scenery grows choppy. Stretches of farmhouses and cemeteries are broken by Zippy Marts, pizza parlors, and video stores, then more pastureland opens.

"It'll be good for your girls to go off to school," Jerry says. "They'll be busy making new friends, seeing new places."

"Oh, Lord, let's not talk about it."

"I know it's hard. But even if you and Steven hadn't split up, everything would have changed. They'd have gone off to school . . . moved on with their lives."

"It's all happening so fast, I can hardly take it all in. Year after year it's the same old same old, and then when you least expect it, everything changes," she says.

"If people don't change, they die inside, a little every day."

Maggie takes up their mantra. "Step by step."

"Inch by inch."

"A slow grizzly death," they say in unison.

"I know a lot of people like that. Lord, I *was* people like that," she says, as they drive past the city limit sign and into Poplar Grove.

4

Betty

. . . .

*Do not cling to events of the past or dwell on what happened long
ago. Watch for the new thing I am going to do. It is happening
already—you can see it now!*

ISAIAH 43: 18–19

Storm clouds have gathered behind the hospital, offering the hope
of cooler weather, but only the hope. Betty's car, when she gets to
it, is hot as a griddle and smells of melted plastic. She rolls down
the windows, starts the engine, and while she waits for the air-
conditioning to cut on, she mentally goes over her what-to-do-
next list.

On the way home she'll stop at Winn-Dixie and get salad fixings
for supper. It's too hot to cook, and she and Mama Dean haven't
had much of an appetite lately, anyway. After they eat, she'll drive
Mama Dean and Etta Rummage to church for the Rebecca Circle
meeting. Miss Rummage, who is seventy-six, has been a lost soul

since her mother died last winter. Since then, Betty and Mama Dean have tried to get her out of the house at least twice a week.

While they're at their meeting, Betty will tidy up the house, run a load of wash, and pay a few bills, until it's time to drive back to the church to pick them up.

Oh, and in her spare time, she'll figure out what to do about Maggie. As if fixing Maggie's life is something she can add to a list.

As she pulls out of the parking lot, onto East Main Street, fat raindrops spatter the windshield. Betty clicks the wipers on low and thinks about what Annie has said. "It isn't your job to fix Maggie's life. You can't fix another person."

That sounded reasonable, was probably even true. But how could a mother stand by and watch her daughter make a mistake she'd regret forever?

Still, that was Annie all over. She was always reading the latest self-help books, sending lists of books for Betty to read, throwing around words like *co-dependent, enabling, self-actualization.*

Betty had found some of the books at the library in the "Addiction–Recovery" aisle. But she'd been so worried someone would see her in that section that she'd left the library without checking out a single book.

As near as she could figure, what used to be called mothering was now called "co-dependent behavior." What was once considered a "good woman" was now an "enabler." And plain, old-fashioned worrying was "obsessing."

It was all so confusing. Last week, on TV, Gloria Steinem had joked about it.

Phil Donahue: "So, what is a co-dependent?"

Gloria Steinem: "A well-socialized woman."

If the experts were confused, how could an average woman stop trying to help/fix other people? Especially, when the woman was a nurse and mother and was raised to think that taking care of everyone was her bounden duty.

By the time Betty pulls into the Winn-Dixie parking lot, the rain is coming down in torrents. She cuts off the ignition and waits in the car for the worst of the storm to pass. While she waits, she thinks about the dream she had two nights ago.

In the dream, she is walking down the hall at home, carrying a crochet hook. A second later, the crochet hook is stuck through her arm, entering just below her elbow and coming out through her upper arm, as if she reached up to straighten her collar and her arm got pinned in that position.

For a minute she just stands there, staring at her arm in disbelief. A moment before everything had been fine. Now, the hook is buried so deeply in her flesh, only the tip of its handle is visible. She grasps the handle and tries to ease it out, but it won't budge. When it dawns on her that the hook's curve could be caught on something—tendon, blood vessel, bone—she feels faint.

Then through her haze she hears a sound coming from the bedroom. "Mama Dean, is that you? I need help!" she cries. Her voice is weak, barely a whisper.

She can see Mama Dean's reflection in the bureau mirror. For some reason her mother is on her hands and knees varnishing the bedroom floor. When she calls out, Mama Dean looks up, confused.

Betty calls again: "Mama, I need help!"

In the mirror, she sees a flash of annoyance cross Mama Dean's face. "For goodness' sake, Betty! I can't hear a thing you're saying. I've painted myself into a corner here, so you'll just have to wait 'til I come out."

Betty eases herself to the floor, feeling fainter by the second.

A moment later the front door bangs open. Three men who look like Smiling Jack come into the room. They are dressed in black wool overcoats and dark fedoras, worn low over their eyes. They walk as a unit, as if they're attached at the shoulders.

"Please! I need help," she says.

The men walk toward her, glance at her arm, then start bickering among themselves, as if she isn't in the room.

"I don't know what they expect us to do," one of the Jack look-alikes says, in a flat monotone voice.

"I don't know what they want from me? I don't even know what hospital her family uses," says another.

"I don't know why any of this should be our problem," says the third.

Then, still joined at the shoulders, they leave the house, banging the door behind them.

The house is silent. Betty is completely alone. Her arm feels cold and numb. It's turning a deep blotchy purple. If the hook has punctured an artery, she could be bleeding to death.

But, she doesn't feel panicky—only a strange detachment, as if the real Betty is floating somewhere near the ceiling watching this other Betty. She wonders if this is how it feels to drown—just resign, give up the struggle, and slowly drift away.

When she surfaces again, a young woman is standing in the doorway. The woman is small and dark and dressed as a nurse. Betty thinks the woman is either Maggie or Annie, though she doesn't really look like either of them.

The woman leans over her.

Betty whispers, "I tried to pull it out, but it's caught . . ."

The woman shakes her head and says matter-of-factly, "Oh, you'll never get it out by yourself. I've come to get you help."

Betty groans, remembering the dream. For two days she has tried to puzzle out its meaning. How had the hook got stuck in her arm in the first place? Why couldn't Mama Dean hear her? Who were the three Smiling Jack look-alikes? The small, dark woman?

Tonight she'd write to Annie again. Tell her about the dream. With all the odd books Annie reads, maybe she can figure it out.

By the time she gets home, Mama Dean has dozed off in front of the television.

Betty relaxes. She has a few minutes to collect herself before she starts supper.

She puts the groceries away, pours a glass of iced tea, and sorts through the mail: a bank statement, a back-to-school sale at Kmart. At the bottom of the stack there's a thick envelope from Annie.

She kicks off her Reeboks and settles in at the table. It's only been a week since she mailed the letter to Annie. Annie would barely have had time to read it, let alone answer it. Betty wonders if she's betrayed Maggie by writing such a letter, worries that Annie will think less of her now. But it's too late. The letter has been sent. She makes her mind go blank and opens the envelope. Inside, there's a computer printout cartoon of three grouchy-looking older women. Under the picture the caption says:

Real women don't have hot-flashes, they have power surges.

Betty smiles and tapes the cartoon on the refrigerator door, next to a snapshot of the Brunch Bunch taken in Annie's mauve and blue kitchen.

She is sorting through the rest of the mail when the telephone rings.

A man's voice says, "EllomyoyspeaktoBettySweet?"

Betty shifts the phone to her other ear. "Sorry," she says. "We must have a bad connection. I can't understand a thing you're saying."

"Oh, sorry, love. May I speak to Betty Sweet?"

It isn't a bad connection after all. Just a strange man with an even stranger accent.

"This is Betty Sweet," she says, in the cool tone she reserves for telemarketers.

"I know you don't know me, but my name's Chaaly Love. I'm one of Annie Shepard's mates from the Brunch Bunch."

Betty concentrates for all she is worth, but she keeps getting lost in his accent. His name is Chaaly. He keeps calling her "love" and he seems to know Annie. "Oh, my! Is Annie all right?" she asks.

"Sorry, love. I didn't mean to scare ya. Annie's fine. Right as rain. It's just, we're having a surprise party for her birthday, and we're hoping you can come."

She hears the words *Annie's all right*. The Brunch Bunch is having a surprise birthday party, and they want her, Betty, to come.

She's still trying to decipher everything else, when he says, "I know Annie's birthday is still weeks away, but we want to surprise her with a photo display as well. You know, pictures of her from the cradle 'til now. You've known her from yonks ago, so we're hoping you'll have some old pictures you're willing to share."

Betty is confused. She *has* known Annie longer than just about anyone, but where in the world is Yonksago? It doesn't help that Mama Dean, who woke up when the phone rang, keeps coming into the kitchen to ask questions.

"You want old photos of Annie?" she says, when some of what he's said sinks in.

"Yes, please."

"From where?"

"What do you mean where?"

"I thought you said . . . uh . . . Yonksago?"

"Yonks ago—oh, sorry, love—years ago. Pictures from as far back as you can manage. Mind you, we'll return them after the party."

Mama Dean, who is still dressed in a polka-dotted roller bonnet and a bathrobe held together with three big safety pins, picks that moment to come through the kitchen. She bangs every cupboard and drawer, rattles the grocery sack, then opens the refrigerator and frowns into the container of chicken salad Betty bought for supper.

Betty takes the phone into the half bath off the kitchen so she can hear what Chaaly is saying.

"Are you still there, then, Betty?"

"Yes," she says. "I'll dig through my albums and see what I can come up with."

"Ah, cheers. Annie has said so much about you, I feel like I already know you. Now we're finally going to meet. Thanks ever so much. Tara, then, Betty."

Later, after she's taken Mama Dean and Miss Rummage to their meeting, Betty removes the snapshot of the Brunch Bunch from the refrigerator door. On the back of the photo, Annie has listed the names of each member. She searches for Chaaly, then realizes his name isn't Chaaly after all. It's Charlie. Charlie Love.

Betty feels like a fool. All her life she's wanted to travel to foreign places, but the first time she speaks to someone with a foreign accent, she gets everything wrong—calls him Chaaly—even imagines he is calling her "love"'when it's really his last name.

She turns the picture over and finds him. He's gray-haired and smiling, holding up a T-shirt emblazoned with the words LIMEYS ARE LOVELY. The light reflecting off his glasses gives him a friendly appearance.

5

The phone at Shirley's Curl & Swirl has been ringing off the wall all day. Maggie sighs as she turns the sign in the window to CLOSED.

It's hard to believe that only a few weeks ago, she'd arrived at the Curl & Swirl to find the shop for sale and Shirley in tears. The shop had been dead as four o'clock, ever since the Beauty Box, with its air guns, blending shears, and vent dryers, had opened at the mall. For a while Shirley had gotten by with running specials and installing a tanning bed. But what her customers really wanted, and what Shirley couldn't supply, were precision haircuts.

"No matter how many classes I take," she'd wailed, "I'm still precision-cut illiterate!"

Then one day, Shirley's prayers were answered. The Beauty Box was hit with a lawsuit.

The *Expositor* column was still thumbtacked to the bulletin board in the breakroom.

Blondelle Asburn says she wanted her hair curled not fried. So she's decided to sue the Beauty Box after most of her hair fell out.

Ms. Ashburn, 45, is suing for $10,000, the maximum the law allows.

According to Ashburn's suit, Jewel Hollifield, a beautician at the Beauty Box, gave her a permanent, but also attended other customers during the process.

"They left it on too long," she said. "When I got home I felt sharp pains in my scalp, but when I tried to rinse it out, my hair just melted and ran down the drain. I was completely bald on the right side. Then, at supper that night, the left side fell out, right into my pinto beans. I liked to have died when that happened."

The Beauty Box, located at the Port City Mall, in Poplar Grove, will be closed until further notice.

An hour after the story broke the Curl & Swirl was returned to its rightful place as the most popular shop in Poplar Grove. And Maggie was hired as the only precision haircutter in town.

Today everyone in the shop had been too busy to take more than one breath at a time. The big fall issue of *Southern Hairdo Magazine*'s main feature was "Soap Opera Stars with Precision Haircuts" and every woman from Landis to Huntersville seemed to want one.

Maggie can't remember the last time she felt so tired. She locks the shop doors, then goes through to her apartment, where she pops a TV dinner into the oven. She has just collapsed onto the tan, nubby couch when she hears a knock on the door.

She gets up and squints through the miniblinds. It's her best friend, Mary Price Bumbalough, staring back at her.

Mary Price, who sings and plays country-western music at the Palomino Club, is dressed in a canary yellow cowgirl suit that matches her canary yellow hair. Just seeing her standing there looking so outrageous makes Maggie feel better.

Mary Price is barely through the door when she says, "They were playing 'You Picked a Fine Time to Leave Me, Lucille' on the car radio. But it just come to me, we've only heard *his* side of the story, so I'm fixing to write a song with Lucille's version. Remember the line about four hungry children and the crops in the field? Well, I started thinking, that's the perfect time to leave. I mean, why would she leave if things were going good?"

Maggie laughs, but Mary Price is so caught up in the story she ignores her. "What if Lucille hated that farm. What if she'd said, 'Please, please, oh please, don't spend our savings on that farm. The land's nothing but clay and rock. There's no electric or indoor plumbing.' But her husband said, 'Don't you ever tell me what to do,' and bought the sorry place.

"Well, Lucille was a good woman, so she did what she thought was her duty. She worked that farm like a field hand. And did her husband appreciate it? Lord, no. Every day he said things like, 'Dammit, Lucille, you'll never get that tree down if you don't throw your back into it.' Or, ' Lord, woman, you ain't worth the powder to blow you up.'"

Mary Price lights up a cigarette and continues. "Then one night on her way to the outhouse she tripped over a stump. Well, the poor thing lay there alone in the dark, her whole life flashing before her eyes. They'd been there for years and still didn't have indoor plumbing. They didn't have electricity either. Her four sons had grown into men as rude and bossy as her husband. When Lucille finally got to her feet, she was thinking about the hungry children and crops. That's what her husband always said to keep her in line. But then it hit her. Her children were grown. The farm and her husband didn't have a thing to do with her anymore. So why was she still there? If they were hungry they could cook. They could harvest the fields, too. Lucille was checking out."

Mary Price flops on the couch and grins. "Honest to God, Maggie, can't you just see it?"

Maggie nods, then feels depressed. "You can sure paint a picture. That husband was clueless. Steven never got it either."

Mary Price smiles. "Clueless. That's the perfect word."

"I tried to tell him for years," Maggie says, "but he wouldn't listen—never heard a thing I said. He just kept doing what he was doing, then went into pure-d shock when I left."

Mary Price shakes her head and slides a pack of Virginia Slims across the couch cushion.

Maggie gets up, closes the miniblinds, then the curtains, and takes one. "I swear, I've been trying to give up smoking, but this is enough to make a person take up smoking full-time. I don't know if this has been the best year of my life or the worst," she says.

Mary Price lights up, too, tossing her burnt-out match somewhere in the vicinity of the ashtray. "Nobody ever said being a rebel is easy."

"Well, maybe I wasn't cut out to be a rebel. I mean, the world needs everyday kind of people too. I figure that's what I am—just an everyday kind of person."

Mary Price stares at her. "Well, it's too late for that. Your days of being everyday were over the minute you laid eyes on Jerry Roberts."

"I know. Jerry's been the best part of my life this year—or any year now that I think about it. But there's still plenty of worsts. Like my girls and Mama Dean not speaking to me. And Mother . . . I don't even know what to say to my own mother."

"If changing a whole life was easy, everyone would do it. But why are you so depressed? The last time we talked it was like you could tackle anything."

Maggie sighs. "I'm just tired. . ."

Neither of them say anything for a while. Finally, Maggie says, "Remember when I told you that right after I left Steven Mama Dean started calling me up and not speaking? She'd call up and just breathe into the phone. At first I thought it was a pervert or something, but she did it so often I started to recognize her breathing."

"Yeah."

"Well, she's doing it again."

"I don't get it. Why would she do such a thing?"

"I don't know for sure. The only thing I can figure is, she thinks if she flat out stops speaking, I'll get used to it and get on with my life. So she calls me up and doesn't speak to *remind* me she's not speaking."

Mary Price narrows her eyes, then grins. "I swear to goodness, you almost have to admire her."

Maggie nods. "Do you want a Co'cola?"

She gets up and goes to the refrigerator. "I always thought leaving Steven would be the hardest part. You know, just getting up the nerve to do the actual leaving. But that's nothing compared to this."

Mary Price follows her to the kitchen. "You're not sorry, are you?"

"No! It's just . . . I know this sounds stupid, but I thought once I left, everything would be perfect."

"You all'd just ride off into the sunset and live happily ever after?"

"Something like that. I just never counted on people not speaking to me, crossing the street when they see me coming, whispering when I pass."

"And that's just your relatives."

"That's another thing that'd be funny if it wasn't the truth," Maggie says, whacking an ice tray on the counter.

"Lord, Maggie, sooner or later it'll blow over," Mary Price says, settling in at the kitchen table.

"When?" Maggie says, filling their glasses.

"I don't know. It's been the slowest summer gossip-wise God ever made. But sooner or later someone's bound to mess up and you'll get put on the back burner. Right now, they're in shock. You have to admit, you and Steven were practically an institution in this town."

"I know."

"Course who wants to live in an institution, right?"

"I swear to you my whole life is flashing before my eyes. I'm not supposed to see Jerry. Steven could make it real ugly if he found out . . . charge me with adultery instead of going for no-fault. In the meantime, I'm working on Main Street, for all the world to see—where anyone who wants to can get at me."

"I hate small towns."

"Everyone knows your business and they all have an opinion."

"You got that right!"

"You know what really gets me? People I thought were my friends priss right past me. Then, people I barely know make it a point to be extra friendly. Course then I wonder if they're just being nice so I'll tell them the real inside story."

"The *National Enquirer* crowd."

"Yeah . . . but it's mostly my family I worry about. I've really hurt my family."

"But you didn't hurt 'em on purpose."

"I know. But even when I knew it would hurt them, I did it anyway."

"Damn, Maggie! Now you're making me depressed."

"What can I say? It *is* depressing."

Mary Price stubs out her cigarette. "Stop it, would you? You're not the first woman in the world to leave her husband and you won't be the last. You can't make everyone happy."

"I tried to love Steven—tried to be what he wanted me to be. I thought that's what love was, trying to be what the other one wanted. When that didn't work, I just pretended everything was fine."

"I couldn't have done it. They'da carried one of us out on a stretcher."

"I pretended because I didn't want anyone to know . . . didn't want to know myself that I'd married a stranger. Steven and I were never right for each other. But try explaining that to Mama Dean. She thinks I'm heading straight for hell."

"Well, she's from the old school. You made your bed and now you have to lie in it."

"Forever and ever, amen."

Maggie stubs out her cigarette, then sprays the room with Lysol. "I let Steven push me around. Maybe it's because I felt guilty for not loving him the way I was supposed to . . . I don't know. I thought if I was nice to him he'd love me for it. But if you marry someone like Steven and go along with whatever they say, they just run all over you."

"And then think you're a fool besides."

"Yeah. The first year we were married, when I wanted to tear out that old, gloomy paneling, Steven said, 'I know you never had much and you've got a lot to learn, but that's GENUINE MAHOGANY PANELING. WE DON'T TEAR OUT GENUINE MAHOGANY PANELING.' He said it slow and drawn out like he thought I was backward, or something."

"What a jerk! You never told me that."

"I didn't tell you because, I don't know . . . I was so young . . . he was so much older than me. I figured he was right. Maybe I did have a lot to learn, maybe I *was* backward or something, so I didn't say anything, I just let him."

"You were right. That paneling made your house dark as a tomb."

"I was only twenty and I already had the girls . . . everyone kept telling me that I was lucky to have him—that he was a good man."

"Just because he's not Jack the Ripper doesn't make him a good man. You were just too young, Maggie. We were both too young."

"Yeah, but at least Hoyt lets you be. I never knew a person could just be—that that should be enough."

Mary Price shrugs. "Hoyt didn't have a choice. I wouldn't have married Elvis himself if he wouldn't let me be."

"You were always smarter than me—more of a fighter. Even when we were kids you never let anyone push you around. I always admired that. I remember you and your mother arguing like sisters—not like mother and daughter. But toe-to-toe arguing like you were both the same age. Like you had as much right to be the boss as she did."

Mary Price looks blank. "I don't remember."

"That's because it was everyday stuff for you."

"Maybe."

"It was. The first time I saw you all fussing, I was shocked. I remember going home and trying it out. You know, talking back to Mother and Mama Dean just to see if I could get by with it. But they put a stop to that in a heartbeat."

"They were strict over the oddest things."

"Yeah."

Mary Price swirls the half-melted ice in her glass. "But I remember thinking it would be sort of neat to live in a house where they expected something from you. Even when we were real little, maybe seven or eight, your mother and Mama Dean made you help around the house. I remember how awful your bed always looked— like some little kid had made it. At my house, my mother went behind me and remade my bed 'til it was perfect. Nothing I did was ever good enough. Lord, here I am, thirty-eight years old and I still don't think I know how to make a bed right. Maybe that's why my house looks like the armpit of the world now."

Maggie smiles, taking it all in. "I always thought your house was so . . . I don't know . . . exotic. Even if you had lunch meat for supper, your mom called it cold cuts. She'd lay them out on a platter lined with lettuce and cheese, just like I imagined New York City deli food. And you had store-bought potato salad and bakery cakes. One Father's Day, you all had a bakery cake decorated like the front of a man's shirt, bowtie and all. I thought that was so great. At my house we had boring homemade cakes. And when I'd spend the night, you all had a couch in the front room that made out into a bed. I'd never seen one before. Your folks would go to bed and we were allowed to stay up as late as we wanted, watching TV from that pull-out bed. All your mom said was, 'If you all stay up too late, you're the ones who'll feel awful in the morning.' I mean, she really seemed to think we were old enough to decide how late was 'too late.' At my house they *told* me when to go to bed."

"Lord, Maggie, why are you remembering all this now?"

Maggie shakes her head. "I don't know. Maybe it's about being . . . being allowed to be who you are. From day one you trusted yourself, like what you thought was as good as what anyone else thought. I never thought what I thought made much of a difference to anyone. They told me what to do and I did it. Maybe that's what makes it harder now . . . you know . . . to go against the rules."

Mary Price blows a smoke ring toward the ceiling. "I always thought rules were made to be broken."

"Me, too. But only by other people. I was always too scared."

Mary Price grins. "Oh, you had your moments."

Maggie leans forward in her chair. "Did I? I don't remember. Tell me what you remember. Anything I did that broke the rules."

"Well, for starters, you stayed friends with me even when your mother and Mama Dean thought I was a bad influence."

Maggie smiles. "I did, didn't I?"

"Yep. And we smoked Kools on the sly and you saw Jerry on the sly."

"I'm glad. I'm glad I did a few things. Can you remember anything else, Mary Price?"

"Well, now, let me think."

Maggie sighs. "There isn't anything else, is there?"

Mary Price looks exasperated. "Well, Lord, Maggie. I'm sorry! If I'd known this was going to be a test, I'd have studied up."

"It's not your fault. Sometimes I just wonder if I got stuck someplace."

"What do you mean 'stuck'?"

"Well, nothing's changed much. Here I am twenty years later, still seeing you, still seeing Jerry, and smoking on the sly."

"Yeah. But at least you've got Jerry."

"Thank goodness for that."

"Yep. Just think how you'd feel if you got stuck in those nineteen years with old Steven."

6

All week, Betty has planned to sort through her old photo albums for pictures of Annie. There are a half-dozen albums on the bottom shelf of her bookcase, dated and organized, but dusty and forgotten. In the hall closet, two hatboxes are filled to the brim with snapshots she's been meaning to organize and put into albums for years.

But it's been a bad week on the Alzheimer's Unit. So bad that *planning* to sort through the albums is as far as she's gotten.

On Monday, Ginny Whisneat, Betty's favorite young nursing assistant, was attacked by a patient. What made it so shocking was that Betty was with them in the day room when it happened and she hadn't seen it coming.

The patient, Mr. Moseley, was new, too, but until the moment of the attack, had been the sweetest, most predictable man on the unit.

It had all happened so fast. One minute Mr. Moseley was smiling serenely over a breakfast of Egg-beaters and prune muffins, the next moment he'd knocked Ginny off balance and wrestled her to the floor.

It had taken three nurses to get him back to his room, but once he was in bed, his smile was as innocent as a baby's. Why, if Ginny hadn't still been sprawled out on the day room floor, Betty would have thought that she'd imagined the whole thing.

Ginny was more stunned than hurt. But there were still strict procedures to follow. Mr. Moseley's doctor and family had to be notified. An incident report had to be written. Then along with their regular duties the entire staff was subjected to mandatory, after-shift lectures on "Managing Your Alzheimer Patient" given by experts who were long on credentials but short on the actual experience of working in a nursing home. Finally, on Friday, a stocky, red-haired woman led a class that applied to real life by showing them how to "diffuse the situation" with a few well-placed self-defense holds.

Betty knows about real life on the third floor—old ladies, bright as new money one minute, then wandering the halls, naked, the next; gentlemanly types like Mr. Moseley, getting a crush on a nurse and suddenly deciding to "take her" caveman style.

Betty has her own theories. She's noticed that when the patients are tired or hungry they are more apt to be confused and angry. When she reads Mr. Moseley's chart, she sees that he'd had a restless night just before his tantrum. Betty understands. Some days she'd like to throw a tantrum herself. Unfortunately, she still has all her inhibitions.

On Friday, the maintenance men, all bustle and belts, arrive with the promise of attaching a security gate to the nurses station—something the nurses have begged for all year. If all else fails, a gate will keep the nurses in and the patients out until help arrives.

All morning, the third floor hums with frayed nerves and electric drills.

Just before two o'clock, Betty is wheeling Mrs. Honeycutt to the day room, when Angie Stutts, a young nursing assistant with spiked blond hair, peeks into the room and hisses, "Betty! Get over here! I swear you will not believe this!"

Betty locks the wheelchair into place, settles Mrs. Honeycutt in front of *As The World Turns*, and follows Angie up the hall to the nurses station, where a crowd has gathered.

Rose Snipes, from housekeeping, nods in their direction, then turns to Lila Proctor from respiratory therapy. "If that ain't the beatingest thing."

"Why, I never in my life saw any such," Lila says.

"I swan, my two-year-old grandson coulda did a better job than that," Rose says.

Angie shakes her head at Betty. "I swear, whoever thought of this has a brain the size of a pea."

Betty stares at the security gate. It has enough hardware to keep out Coxey's Army, but the gate itself is only knee-high.

They are still standing at the nurses station, wondering what in the world, when one of the patients steps over the gate and joins them.

It's Saturday, Betty's day off, before she finally carries the hatbox of pictures into her bedroom and empties the contents on the bed.

She plans to be methodical, to focus only on the pictures of Annie for the surprise party. But before she knows it, hours have passed, and she's still sitting cross-legged in the middle of the bed, surrounded by hundreds of pictures.

There's one of Mama Dean, at nine, in pigtails and a plaid dress, gazing solemnly into the camera. Then a formal studio portrait of her parents, taken shortly after their wedding. Mama Dean is wearing a traveling suit. She looks touchingly young and dreamy-eyed as she leans expectantly toward the camera. Her father, Donley Pruitt, is wearing a tweed cap and belted suit that reminds Betty of pictures of F. Scott Fitzgerald. His mouth curves upward, but there is a wistful look in his eyes as he stares past the camera into the distance.

Betty carries the picture to the window to examine it more closely. Maybe something in their young faces will reveal what went wrong—why the marriage ended so badly. But the picture doesn't yield a single clue—nothing in their expressions gives any warning of what's to come.

Betty goes out to the kitchen for a cup of coffee. Mama Dean is sitting at the table, holding the telephone receiver to her ear. When she sees Betty, she gets an odd look on her face and hangs up the phone with a crash.

"Sorry, Mama. I didn't mean to scare you. I didn't hear you talking," Betty says, on her way to the coffeemaker.

Mama Dean glares at her. "I . . . uh . . . wasn't . . . talking. I was just fixing to call Etta . . . remind her about bingo tonight at the new Super Kmart."

"Well, don't let me hold you up," Betty says. "I'll take my coffee back to my room. What time do you all need me to drive you?"

"What?" Mama Dean says, looking confused.

"To bingo tonight."

"What about bingo tonight?"

"You just said you were calling Miss Rummage about bingo tonight."

Mama Dean glares again. "Watch how you talk to me, sister. I'm still your mother!"

"Lord, Mama, I was just asking."

"Hmmp."

"Oh, never mind. All I'm saying is, after you talk to Miss Rummage just let me know what time. All right?"

Mama Dean doesn't say anything. She just folds her arms across her chest and gives Betty her steeliest "shoot-if-you-must-this-old-gray-head" look.

Betty thinks about the past week on the Alzheimer's Unit and wonders if it's her destiny to be surrounded by contrary, confusing people. Honestly, Mama Dean was getting more contrary and confusing every day! Back in her room, she attacks the pictures, sorting through them quickly. She makes a stack of Maggie's photos, a separate pile of Mama Dean's, and another of herself.

She finds a snapshot from nineteen forty-five. She and Annie, at seventeen, are hamming it up for the camera at the Greyhound bus station in Statesville. They're leaving Poplar Grove with Moose Club scholarships for the Raleigh School of Practical Nursing. Betty smiles at the memory. It was exciting enough to be leaving home for the first time. But Raleigh! Rumor had it that *anything* could happen in Raleigh.

She finds another photo of them, a year later, dressed in their nurses uniforms and caps, proudly waving their diplomas. There are several pictures of Annie without her—a black-and-white high school graduation picture, a formal wedding photograph, along with the yellowed newspaper clipping of the event. Later, Christmas card photos of Annie and Ed with their children.

Betty chooses six of the most flattering and slips them into an envelope.

Tonight, after supper, when she takes Mama Dean and Miss

Rummage to bingo, she'll drop the photos at Eckerd's and get copies for Charlie Love.

She is putting the boxes back on the closet shelf when an Eckerd photo envelope falls to the floor. She opens it and finds pictures taken weeks before at her granddaughters' graduation party. Amy looks cool and confident in her graduation gown and pearls. Jill, dressed like Hiawatha, makes a peace sign with one hand and waves her diploma with the other. Beside them, Maggie and Steven are smiling like typical proud parents.

It's still hard to believe that the very next day Maggie let herself out the door.

Betty's stomach churns and she decides not to think about it now. Instead, she takes a deep breath, puts the envelope back in the hatbox, and closes the closet door.

A moment later, she heads to the kitchen to start lunch. Mama Dean is still sitting at the table with the telephone receiver pressed to her ear. Betty pauses, taking it all in. Mama Dean isn't saying anything and there's something suspicious about her silence—the way she's hunched over the phone. Then Betty remembers that when she went to the kitchen for coffee, earlier, Mama Dean had slammed down the phone.

That's when it hits her. "For goodness' sakes, Mama. You're calling people up and not speaking, aren't you?"

7

Maggie

"Well, Maggie," Steven says. "I can't stop you from trying to see the girls, but I can't guarantee that they'll be here when you get here."

Maggie is quiet. Static crackles over the line while she tries to think of something to say. His words, dripping with sarcasm, buzz inside her head. For nineteen years, she'd been bullied by that voice. Now all she wants to do is slap his insolent face.

She remembers raising the girls alone while Steven chaired every committee in town. The promises he made, but didn't keep, because something more important always came up. His ugly, cutting remarks when they couldn't live up to his impossible standards. All those years she'd walked on eggs, trying to reassure the girls but, at the same time, trying not to say anything that would make them think less of him.

Now, Steven is in the catbird seat. He can control when and if she sees her daughters by deciding whether or not to tell them she's called. He can lie like a rug if he wants to and she's completely at his mercy.

She feels the heat rise up her neck. It's true what they say about getting hot under the collar. Finally she says, "It would be better for the girls if we try to be friendly."

Steven is silent.

After several long seconds, she says, "All right, Steven. I'll call back later . . ."

But before she can finish her sentence the line hums. Steven has hung up.

She slams down the phone and crashes around the apartment, cursing so loudly that she finally shocks herself into silence.

Later, after she's had a good, long cry, she wonders why she'd even tried to speak to Steven. The minute she'd heard his voice her gut reaction was to hang up. She'd forced herself to speak because she thought it was the adult thing to do. Now, she remembers a quote Mary Price had read from one of the magazines at the Curl & Swirl. "Doing the same thing over and over again, but expecting a different outcome, is the sign of insanity."

They'd laughed when they'd read it. But she should have cross-stitched it on a pillow. For her, the definition of insanity was trying to talk to Steven. In all their years together they'd never been able to talk anything through. Why did she think that he'd be more reasonable now that she'd left him?

Well, she is sick of his bullshit. She doesn't have to play his games anymore. She might have to call the house, but if *he* answers, the only game she'll play is Mama Dean's. She'll call up and not speak, keep calling and not speaking until one of the girls finally answers.

There are several gift-wrapped packages stacked on the kitchen table. She'd saved tip money for weeks for backpacks, stationery, and rolls of stamps for the girls. Then a pink cashmere-like sweater for Amy and turquoise earrings for Jill. She had planned to surprise them with an evening of presents and pizza.

She knew she couldn't settle everything between them in one evening, but it seemed like a good place to start.

But then Steven had answered the phone and ruined everything.

She flips on the radio, then goes to the bathroom to splash cold water on her eyes. She paints up a little, then spikes up her hair for courage.

When she comes out of the bathroom, Elton John's "I'm Still Standing" is playing on the radio. She decides it's a sign.

A few minutes later, she loads the gifts into the trunk, then drives down East Main, past the Dairy Queen, the library, and Jolene's Skating Rink. Her daughters have to be somewhere in this town. She'll keep driving around until she finds them.

As she pulls into the Dixie Burger parking lot, she daydreams about driving to the old house, parking her car out front, and waiting for them to come home. Steven would glare at her from behind the dark velvet drapes, but there wasn't much else he could do. She'd sit there just to irritate him, daring him to come out and confront her.

Used to be, she'd rather take a beating than to risk a scene in public. But half the town already thinks she's ruined, the other half that she's crazy. She has nothing to lose. Steven, who likes to think of himself as a pillar of the community, has plenty to lose. He might bully his wife in private, but he'd hand over his daughters when a crazy woman came calling, threatening to make their private life public.

Maggie jerks herself back to reality as Amy, then Jill come out of Dixie Burger. She's hit the jackpot. The girls, who never go anywhere together, are actually at the same place, at the same time. This has to be a sign too.

As she waves to them, she files the daydream somewhere in the back of her mind, under the heading FUTURE REFERENCE—STEVEN'S WORST NIGHTMARE.

But her victory is short-lived. The minute the girls spot her, they duck back inside the restaurant.

It's probably only seconds, but it feels like several long minutes while she debates whether to drive off as if none of this is happening or to pull her rank as Mama by barging into the restaurant and dragging the girls outside.

But she's too busy concentrating on breathing to decide anything. A few minutes later, the girls emerge, whisper something to each other, scan the parking lot, then start slowly toward the car. Maggie's chest feels tight as she watches them. Amy, all color-coordinated and perfect, looks bored. Jill, who is dressed in ragged blue jean cut-offs and a faded, tie-dyed T, looks pale and thin.

"Hey, girls, I've been looking all over town for you." Even to her own ears, her voice sounds forced, unnaturally high.

The girls stand at the car window, staring down at their feet, avoiding her eyes.

"Get in," she says. "I bought you a few things . . . thought we could go to my place and order pizza . . . spend the evening together. We'll call Daddy from there so he'll know where you are . . . "

Even before she sees them roll their eyes with their, Lord-give-us-strength-with-fools-and Mama-look, she knows she is rattling on and on. But somehow she can't seem to stop herself.

"Come on, get in."

The girls scan the parking lot again. Maggie wonders if they're embarrassed to be seen with her or if they're hoping someone will come along and rescue them. Either way, it is not a good sign. She's just starting to wonder if they're going to spend all of eternity, shuffling from foot to foot on the blacktop, when they open the door and climb into the backseat.

She pulls onto East Main, past Jolene's Skating Rink, the library, and the Dairy Queen. She tries to pretend that this is an ordinary day, that the tension in the car is typical of mothers and teenagers everywhere. But the girls still haven't said the first word and her head is beginning to throb.

"So, what have you been up to?" she asks.

"Nothing," they say in unison.

"Nothing? I can't believe you haven't been busy, what with getting ready for school and all . . . I'm dying to hear everything . . . when we get to my place, we'll have a real talk."

She parks behind the apartment and gets out of the car, but the girls don't move. They just sit there in the backseat, staring straight ahead. Finally she says, "Come on, girls. We're here."

They climb out of the car and follow her to the door, sighing louder than she'd thought was humanly possible.

She unlocks the door, then remembers the gifts. "Go on in. Make yourselves at home. I left something in the car."

When she returns a moment later, they are still standing in the foyer, exactly where she'd left them. This is getting worse and worse. She presses on. "Come on. Sit down. Do you all want a Co'cola? I've got Coke and tea . . . oh, and Dr Pepper. You like Dr Pepper, don't you, Jill?"

Jill doesn't look at her. "I don't care," she mumbles.

Maggie goes to the kitchen to call Steven. Thank heaven he isn't at home. She leaves a message on his machine, then orders the pizza—Meat-Lover's Thin Crust—the girls' favorite. She can hear them whispering in the next room, but she can't make out any of their words. Her palms are sweating. She wipes her hands on the legs of her jeans, then, as she pours the soda, she strains toward the living room. The girls are silent.

As she rounds the corner, she panics. She imagines they've sneaked out while she poured the drinks, she expects to find the room empty.

But they're still slumped on the sofa, staring straight ahead.

Calm down, she tells herself. Stop thinking the worst. Stop rattling on and on or you *will* run them off. Still, it's almost impossible not to rattle on and on, when hers is the only voice filling the silence.

She sets the glasses on the coffee table, then returns to the kitchen for the gifts. She hands them the packages. "I got you a few things for school. I hope you like 'em."

She'd shopped so carefully—the sweater is Amy's favorite shade of pink. She remembered Jill admiring the turquoise earrings in the window of Willard's. The backpacks, stationery, and rolls of stamps had taken the last of her savings, but she'd been sure it would be worth it when she saw the looks on their faces.

Now, as they open gift after gift, their faces go from pinched to stony and back again. Suddenly the room seems as hot and airless as the inside of a closet. Tears sting her eyes. Hoping the girls haven't noticed, she hurries to the kitchen. She'd known that none of this would be easy, but now she almost comes apart. She's longed for this evening—dreamed about it for weeks, convinced herself that it was possible to make peace with her daughters before they went off to college—maybe out of her life forever.

Now she's hiding out in the kitchen, taking deep gulping breaths and running the water full force so they won't hear her.

When she turns off the faucet, she hears whispers, then a door slams.

She rushes back to the room. Jill, who is standing near the coffee table, whirls around to face her.

"Where's Amy?"

"She left."

"What happened?"

Jill's eyes flash. "For God's sake, Mama, what did you expect? I'm getting out, too, before I say the wrong thing."

"Oh, Lord, Jill, don't go. Say anything you want. We need to talk. To fight if we have to. Just don't go. I can't stand the thought of you going off with nothing settled between us."

"What did you expect? We don't hear from you for weeks, then you practically snatch us from a parking lot, bring us to . . . this . . . this place, bribe us with gifts and pizza. God, Mama, that won't settle anything."

"That's not fair! I've called the house dozens of times . . . left messages . . . I didn't know you didn't get them . . . "

"That's bull and you know it, Mama. You coulda found us. You managed to find us today. No, you just stay in your precious apartment. I hope you'll be very happy."

Maggie lifts her hands as if warding off a blow. "Stop it! I've wanted to talk to you . . . to explain. But when I didn't hear from you, I figured that you didn't want to talk to me . . . I thought you needed time."

Jill ducks her head. Her voice is faint, barely a whisper. "I can't believe any of this. That you'd do this to us."

"I can't believe it either. But Daddy and I hadn't gotten along for years. You know that." Maggie reaches out and touches her daughter's arm.

Jill jerks away. "Don't blame this on Daddy! *He* didn't run off."

Maggie's voice is pleading. "I didn't plan to run off. It was the last thing I wanted. Daddy and I had a fight. I was upset. People get upset, Jill. They do things they didn't plan."

Jill's eyes blaze. "Well, excuse me. Excuse the hell out of me. I guess I thought we were enough . . . that me and Amy were enough . . . that you'd stay for us."

"You and Amy are getting out as fast as you can. How can you expect me to stay if you can't wait to get out?" Maggie gasps, shocked at what she's said.

Jill rushes past her toward the door.

But Maggie gets there first and blocks it.

"Move, Mama."

"Jill, I'm sorry. I shouldn't have said that. He's your father and you love him. That's only right. But, I'm your mother. Whatever happens between Daddy and me, don't ever think I don't love you."

She stares into Jill's eyes, reaches out her hand. But in that instant, Jill pushes past her and is out the door.

8

Betty is beginning to feel that she lives in a world of pop quizzes and all her answers are wrong.

Monday morning, the nursing home has a fire drill. When the loudspeaker blares, "Code red!" Betty is in room 301 sponge-bathing Mrs. Blankenship, who is bedridden.

The rule was that you cleared the hall of any obstacles and herded the patients behind the fireproof doors near the day room. Betty covers Mrs. Blankenship and wheels her to safety. On the way back, she pushes the food cart flat against the wall and sets an empty tray on top. A moment later, she captures two wandering old ladies. Then, she sprints back to 301, where she finds Mrs. Honeycutt, Mrs. Blankenship's roommate. Except for a string of red beads around her neck, Mrs. Honeycutt is naked. Betty helps her into her robe and wheels her up the hall. But the instant she opens the door, the two wandering ladies get out.

That's the trouble with fire drills, she thinks. They're like trying to catch a school of minnows with bare hands. Angie Stutts arrives just in time to nab the wandering ladies, and Betty darts back to double-check the day room. She spots Mr. Moseley huddled under a table. She puts her arms around him and croons, "You Are My Sunshine, My Only Sunshine." The song soothes him and he allows her to lead him. But when she opens the door, Angie is trying to separate the wandering ladies, who are fighting over Mrs. Honeycutt's red beads. Mrs. Blankenship is screaming that Mrs. Honeycutt stole the beads from her in the first place. And Mrs. Honeycutt hangs on to the beads for all she is worth, while making odd yipping noises that remind Betty of toy poodles.

In all the confusion Mr. Moseley opens the door and makes a run for it.

Betty catches up with him, just as the all-clear buzzer sounds, and Fayette Chupp, of all people, appears from around a corner. Fayette and Betty have worked together for thirty years. But now that Fayette has been promoted to third-floor supervisor she looks at Betty as if she's never laid eyes on her before. Fayette has also taken to wearing a seventies-style starched white uniform and cap, she carries a massive key ring, a flashlight the size of a billy-club, and a clipboard for documenting the slightest infraction. She seems to think this makes her look important, that it sets her apart from the other nurses who wear white slacks, T-shirts, and sneakers. It sets her apart all right. Behind her back, the nicest thing anyone calls her is Nurse Ratchet.

But what really flies all over Betty is, since the promotion, Fayette makes Betty call her Mrs. Chupp, while she still calls Betty Betty.

Fayette sniffs. "Betty, you do know we're having a fire drill?"

"Yes, it's just . . ." Betty stammers. For some reason she is out of breath. And it's not just because of the fire drill and running after Mr. Moseley. It's because no matter how hard she works, Fayette always manages to make her feel that she's done something wrong.

Fayette holds up her hand, cutting Betty off midsentence. "A fire drill is serious business in a nursing home."

"I know that—"

"Excuse me!"

"I know that, Mrs. Chupp. We got everyone behind the fire door, but Mr. Moseley slipped off."

"It's your job to see that things like that never happen."

Betty holds her breath. It's on the tip of her tongue to say, "Hey, Fayette. Bite my butt!" and it shocks her. She's never said these words before. Not out loud. Not even in her head. She'd heard it someplace. A TV program? Angie and Ginny fooling around in the day room? Only one look at Fayette's fat fingers clutching the clipboard had stopped her, reminded her that Fayette would like nothing better than to write her up.

After Fayette stalks off, Betty stands there blinking, while Mr. Moseley hums tunelessly. It isn't until he pats her on the shoulder that she realizes he is humming "You Are My Sunshine, My Only Sunshine."

Betty is relieved to be home in one piece. She pulls into the driveway, parks the car, and sits there wishing she'd taken a longer way home. She needs reentry time—a few minutes to pull herself together before she can face Mama Dean. For weeks they've been fussing and arguing, and today, she's already used up her last good nerve.

When she sees the curtains in the front room move, she gets out of her car and goes into the house. She is barely through the door when Mama Dean, who is sitting in the rocking chair by the window, says, "Well, I swan. Look what the cat's done drug in."

"Lord, Mama. I'm only ten minutes late, and after the day I've had—"

Mama Dean cuts her off midsentence. "Leave it to you to be off gallivanting the one night I need to be someplace."

The word "gallivanting" flies all over Betty. She can't remember the last time she gallivanted. She never goes anywhere but to work, church, or the Winn-Dixie.

She takes a deep breath. Mama Dean is spoiling for a fight. But she isn't going to rise to the bait. Instead, she stomps off to the bathroom and splashes her face with cold water until she's pretty sure she won't have a stroke. When she calms down, she changes out of her uniform and into shorts and a T-shirt.

In an hour, she'll drive Mama Dean and Etta Rummage to the church. The Rebecca Circle is having a housewarming, potluck supper for Ada Jennings, who is moving two miles down the road to the Oaks Retirement Village.

For the first time in weeks, Betty will have an evening to herself.

She sighs and goes back to the front room. Mama Dean is still sitting at the window, still dressed in an old robe and roller bonnet. "Well, Mama," Betty says. "Here you are fussing at me when you're not even dressed."

Mama Dean says, "Hmmmph," but goes to her room. She returns a few minutes later wearing a blue flowered church dress and white Reeboks along with the polka-dotted roller bonnet.

Betty decides not to mention the Reeboks. "You can't wear that old roller bonnet to church. You'll look like a haint. Here, let me fix your hair."

Mama Dean crosses her arms over her chest and pooches out her bottom lip.

Betty brushes her hair, then dabs on a trace of pink lipstick, while Mama Dean twists in her chair like a child with a head full of tangles.

"Stop, Betty! Stop fussing."

A few minutes later, they pick up Miss Rummage, then drive on to East Main, past Wynette's Flower Shop and the new foreign bakery. When they stop at the light in front of the bank, Betty notices that the car ahead of them has a bumper sticker that says: DOING MY BEST TO PISS OFF THE RELIGIOUS RIGHT.

Betty's heart sinks. If Mama Dean sees the sticker they will never hear the end of it. But for the first time all day, luck is with her. A woman in a too-short skirt is setting up a back-to-school display in Woolworth's window, and while Mama Dean and Miss Rummage are busy being scandalized by this, the light changes and the car with the bumper sticker speeds off.

By the time Betty drops them off at the church, she's as limp as a dishrag.

On the way home, on impulse, she pulls into Dixie Burger. It's too hot to cook, and since Mama Dean doesn't approve of fast food, this small act of defiance feels like a treat.

She had planned to spend the evening catching up on the laundry and housework, but as she turns into the driveway, she decides to spend the next couple of hours treating herself.

Instead of her usual shower, she'll take a long soak. She fills the tub, scenting the water with the lavender bubble bath Maggie gave her for Mother's Day. If she wants to spend all evening lounging in the tub, that's exactly what she'll do.

As she sinks into the water, she thinks about Mama Dean accusing her of gallivanting. Well, she didn't gallivant. She's never gallivanted a day in her life. But now she is more determined than ever to go to Annie's party. If that's what Mama Dean thinks of her, she might as well gallivant on down to the beach. Why, she'd spend a whole week with Annie without a single trace of guilt.

An hour later, she's standing in front of a full-length mirror, trying on the new dress she bought just in case she ever went anywhere. The radio is playing Jim Croce's "Bad, Bad, Leroy Brown." She moves her bare feet, watches her skirt sway to the music and wonders about Annie's party. Except for the hospital Christmas party she hasn't been to a party for years. At least not one with grown-ups of both sexes. She thinks about Charlie Love. It's embarrassing to admit it, even to herself, but ever since he'd called and she'd heard his English acccent, she's been thinking about him. She's even reading her old Agatha Christies again and watching British mysteries on PBS. At first she couldn't understand a word any of them said, but now they were her favorites. Even the one with that crotchety lawyer, Rumpole.

A knock at the back door jerks her back to the present.

She turns down the radio, hoping she's imagined the sound.

But the knocking continues.

She wants to hide—to pretend no one's home. She's looked forward to this evening—just thinking about this time alone had kept her going all week.

"Why can't I get a moment's peace?"she mutters, as she starts up the hall toward the kitchen.

When she opens the door, Maggie is standing on the back porch, crying her eyes out.

9

After Jill ran out of the apartment, Maggie couldn't seem to get enough air. Everything was happening too fast, falling apart when it's supposed to be coming together.

Without thinking about what she's doing, she gets in her car and drives straight to her mother's.

But when Betty answers the door there's a look of surprise and confusion on her face and Maggie sees all the weeks and changes that have come between them. Then, she flings herself into her mother's arms.

"Oh, Maggie, what have you gone and done?"

"Oh, Mama. I've lost my babies."

The next thing she knows, they are on the couch. Her mother is holding her and she's weeping, pouring out the details of the meeting with her daughters.

She feels her mother stiffen and pull away. "You bought them presents instead of telling them why you left?"

"They're going off to school. I didn't know where else to start."

Betty's face is pale. "So, it's better to have school clothes, but no explanation . . . all these weeks without a mother and no explanation at all?"

Maggie ducks her head. "I feel bad enough, Mama. You don't have to tell me I messed up."

"It hurts my heart seeing you torn up like this. But you ran off without a word to anyone. What did you expect?"

"Do you think I planned it? Do you think I woke up one day and said, Today I think I'll go out and ruin everyone's lives."

Betty sighs. "I don't know. I don't know what to think anymore."

Maggie is stung. "Lord, Mama, it wasn't like that. *I'm* not like that. The night I left, the girls were in Chapel Hill at Grandmother Presson's. When they got back, I tried to call them . . . left dozens of messages. Then one day it hit me. Steven wasn't giving them my messages. By then, so much time had passed, I didn't know where to start."

"Come on, Maggie. Steven's a good man. He wouldn't do a thing like that."

"Oh, you don't know. That's exactly what he'd do. Just because he isn't a criminal doesn't mean he's a good man."

Betty sits very straight in her chair. "Sometimes," she says, her voice flat. "Sometimes, I just want to hug you and shake you at the same time."

Maggie nods, taking it all in. That was just how she felt about her own daughters. Tonight, she'd wanted to hug them and shake them all at the same time. She just never thought her calm, orderly mother felt the same way about her.

Betty is on her feet now. "I need tea. I'll get us some iced tea," she says, as she heads toward the kitchen.

Maggie leans into the sofa and squeezes her eyes shut. At night, when she can't sleep, she dreams about her new life. She and Jerry are married. Steven doesn't exist. Amy, Jill, Mother, and Mama Dean are happy. In her new life, everyone is happy.

Betty sets their glasses on the coffee table, then presses her fingers to her temples, bringing Maggie back to reality. "Can't you and Steven get counseling—do whatever it takes to get through this. You've been together so long."

"I stuck it out, Mama. I just stuck it out."

"Oh, Maggie. What a thing to say."

Maggie's voice is matter-of-fact. "It's true. Being married to Steven was killing me."

Betty stares straight ahead, her voice low. "Then you're not going back."

"I'm not going back."

"Tell me. Tell me why you did it, how you could do it?"

Maggie takes a deep breath. "I thought you of all people would get it. I mean, leaving a husband does run in the family."

Betty's jaw clenches and her eyes well up. "Are you trying to hurt me? Did you come here tonight just to hurt me?"

Maggie is on the edge of her seat. "I'm not trying to hurt you. I'm trying to explain." She takes another deep breath, struggles to collect her thoughts. "It's like you spend all those years—thousands of days just barely getting by—and then one day something happens, and you know nothing is ever going to change, and suddenly you know if you don't get out you're going to shrivel up and die."

Betty looks at her, then away. "You never said . . . you never told me you were that unhappy."

Maggie doesn't know why, but suddenly she's angry. "I learned that from you, Mother. We talked every day, but we never said anything. Not really. Not anything important. You divorced Daddy and you never explained. I'm thirty-eight years old and I'm still waiting for an explanation. But no one seems to care about that."

Her mother looks as if this is breaking her heart. She reaches out and places her hand on Maggie's."Oh, Maggie . . . all those years. I'm so sorry."

"I shouldn't have said that. I'm sorry. Sorry for everything. But I need you to understand. I need your support."

Betty sighs. "I want to understand. It's just too much to take in in one night."

Jerry floats into Maggie's mind. There is so much more she needs to tell her mother. She wants to say that she's in love with Jerry Roberts—has loved him for more than half of her life—that soon, very soon, they'd be married. And if she was sure of anything in this world working out, she'd have told her. But they're both exhausted by everything that's already been said.

Betty pats her hand. "I'm glad you came. We needed to talk— make some kind of start."

"Me too. I love you, Mother."

Betty sighs. "I love you, too, baby."

They are still sitting side by side, sighing and staring, when the telephone rings.

Betty shakes her head, then hurries into the kitchen. For the first time Maggie notices that instead of her usual sneakers, her mother is in her bare feet. She's also wearing a flowing print dress instead of her usual uniform. Why, tonight, she even smells different. Instead of Jergens Lotion, her mother smells like lavender.

A moment later, Betty rushes back into the room. "Mama

Dean's on the warpath. I'm late picking her up from church. Do you want to ride with me?"

Maggie shivers. "Mama Dean on the warpath! That's the last thing I need."

"You and me both," Betty says.

"She's giving you fits, isn't she? Fits about me?"

"Yes," Betty says quietly.

Maggie ducks her head. "I'm sorry. I'm just . . . I'm not ready to see her. Not yet. But will you call me sometime?"

"You can't put it off forever. She is your grandmother, you know. Sooner or later you'll have to face her."

"Oh, Lord, Mother. I'd rather take a beating than face her."

"I know. But, if you're going to go through with this, facing Mama Dean's part of it. But I will call you . . . I'll call you from work."

Betty is digging through her purse for her car keys when the phone rings again. "Oh, Maggie, answer it for me."

Maggie starts toward the kitchen, then panics as she lifts the receiver. What will she do if it's Mama Dean again?

But it isn't Mama Dean's voice that stuns her into silence. Instead, it's a man with an accent, saying, "HelloloveisthisBetty?"

Maggie puts her hand over the receiver and whispers, "Mother, it's a man."

Betty takes the phone. "Oh, Charlie, how are you? Listen, I can't talk right now. Is it all right if I call you back?" Then she scratches a number on the tablet near the phone, picks up her purse and car keys, and heads toward the door.

Maggie stands there staring, with her mouth dropped opened. A man with a voice like . . . like James Bond has called and her mother seems to know him—calls him Charlie—acts as if British men named Charlie call every day of the week. Maggie is as shocked as if an alien had fallen out of the sky and landed in her mother's kitchen.

"Mother?"

But Betty stops only long enough to give her a quick hug, then rushes past her, out the door. "I've got to go, Maggie. Mama Dean'll be having a hissy. I'll call you."

Maggie follows her outside and watches her drive off. Then she stands in the driveway for a long time, blinking, wondering about her mother's life. She always thought she knew her mother, knew her through and through. But tonight Betty was wearing a flowing print dress, and talking on the phone to a man Maggie has never met. Now she wonders if anyone ever really knows anyone. She'd never thought of her mother as a woman, let alone an attractive, single woman. She was her mother for the Lordsake. Her own little mama who hadn't had a date since she married Daddy at nineteen. When she wasn't being Mother, she was Mama Dean's daughter or Betty the nurse. Her life was as simple as that, as uncomplicated as that. But tonight, for the first time, Maggie wonders if Jerry is right. Maybe her mother does have this whole secret life no one ever suspected.

It isn't until the streetlights come on that she realizes how late it is. Oh, Lord. Mama Dean will be home any minute! She gets into her car and drives off in a dead panic.

By the time she pulls up behind her apartment, she's completely worn out. But she sits in the car for a long time. She's not ready to go inside yet, not ready to face the girls' drink glasses, or the gifts on the sofa, where they'd left them in their hurry to get away from her.

Now, the snug little apartment she's been so proud of feels as tainted as a crime scene, cluttered with all the evidence of her messed-up life.

She pulls out of the parking lot, then onto East Main and Townsend Avenue. She passes the city limits sign, the That'lldu Bar and Grill, the Farmer's Market, then under a bridge spray-painted with the warning JESUS OR HELL. Within seconds there are rolling hills, dotted with clover. Cattle graze on the hillside. She rolls down her window. The air is sweet and thick. She can feel it on her skin. A minute later she passes Modine Dingler's old farmhouse, then Belews Pond, where she and Jerry had gone to neck back in high school. She turns on to Chatham Road, and as she rounds the corner, she sees Jerry's homeplace, his pickup in the driveway.

For the first time all day it's as if she's come home.

10

"Hello, Charlie. This is Betty. I hope I'm not calling too late."

"Not at all, love. I just rang to thank you for the photos. They're smashing."

Mama Dean, who refused to speak all the way home from church and has sulked in her room ever since, picks that moment to holler, "Betty, where are you? I can't find the remote control."

Betty ignores her. "I think it's so nice what you're doing, giving Annie a surprise party and all."

"Ah, well, Annie's a love. We all had brunch at her place on Sunday. She mentioned your name and I almost blurted out that we'd talked on the phone."

"Oh, no!"

"I caught myself in time, though. I don't think she suspects anything. For some reason this birthday is worrying her. She keeps saying, "How did this happen? How could I, Annie Shepard, possibly be fifty-seven?"

Betty flinches as the *Bonanza* theme blasts from the front room.

She squeezes her eyes shut and ducks into the half bath off the kitchen to get away from the sound. "It's funny," she says, "the way birthdays hit you sometimes."

"I know. You go along for years, not feeling any different than you did at thirty or forty. Then one day you start adding things up and you realize your kids are thirty or forty. Did you and your husband have a big family, Betty?"

Now Mama Dean is channel-surfing. Betty hears canned laughter—Lucy Ricardo shouting, "Oooh, Ricky!" A moment later Rod Serling invites her to enter *The Twilight Zone*.

She shuts the bathroom door. "Just the one. A daughter. He was in Korea when she was born. Annie drove us home from the hospital. That's how long we've been friends. I'll never forget it—Annie looked like a little girl, pulling up in front of the hospital in a big borrowed car. We were both nineteen. Our husbands were overseas. And here I was with a baby. But I guess when you're that young, you think whatever you're doing is normal."

"You don't know at that age, do you? I joined the Navy, said I was eighteen when I was sixteen. I wanted a life of adventure on the high seas. Must have worried my poor mum to death."

"I know. I worried my mother, too. But I wanted to be independent—stay in Raleigh with Annie. We shared an apartment—worked opposite shifts at the hospital so one of us was always with Maggie—that's my daughter. It all worked out. Except for Jack and me, that is. After the war, we didn't work out. But I always wanted a bigger family."

"Me, too. I wish we'd had a bigger family, too. We had two—two boys. After my wife died, Ian, that's our eldest, moved to California. Our Bryan joined the Air Force. He was stationed in England for years, but now he's back in North Carolina."

"I can't imagine that. Maggie and I have always lived in the same town," she says, but she's thinking: He's single. I've let him know I'm single. We both have grown children, so we're around the same age.

"You must enjoy that, having her so close," he says.

Betty takes a deep breath. It is one thing to tell him her whole life, but in a minute she'll be blurting out Maggie's whole life. Being on the phone with a nice, talkative man is making her reckless. She changes the subject. "How did you end up in North Carolina?"

"I was in Korea, too. That's where I met my wife. She was with the Red Cross and from Charlotte. After the war we settled here. That was thirty-odd years ago."

There's a knock on the bathroom door.

"So," Charlie says. "I hope you can come to Annie's party."

There is another knock on the door. This time Betty sighs and says, "I'm sorry. Can you hold on a second?"

She puts her hand over the receiver and opens the door. Mama Dean is standing there, dressed in her old robe and roller bonnet. But now, Mama Dean has added a new twist—one that could send Betty to the hospital's quiet room before bedtime. Mama Dean is drinking pickle juice from a jar of Mount Olive Gherkins. Mama Dean, who shrugs off Dr. Pinckney's advice and ignores everything her daughter the nurse says, considers it gospel when a *National Enquirer* headline screams: MEDICAL BREAKTHROUGH MIRACLE— RUSSIAN SCIENTISTS CLAIM PICKLE JUICE CURES ARTHRITIS.

Mama Dean stares at her. "What're you doing in the bathroom?"

"I'm on the phone, Mama. I couldn't hear myself think with the TV blaring."

"Hmmph," Mama Dean says. "Well, we're almost out of pickles. I need you to pick me up some more tomorrow."

Mama Dean carries the pickle jar into the front room and Betty stands there blinking as this long, crazy day washes over her. Then it hits her. She's spent the last thirty-four years putting her life on hold—waiting for things to settle down, waiting for things to be normal. But tonight, for the first time, she sees that this is it. This is her life. All she needs, all she ever really needed, is a new definition of normal.

"Charlie, I'm sorry that took so long," she says.

"Is everything all right, love?"

"It was my mother. I have this very odd mother who couldn't wait another minute to tell me that pickles cure arthritis."

"Pardon?"

"Well, pickle juice really. She thinks it'll cure arthritis. I told you she was odd."

Charlie laughs. "Eccentric," he says.

"What?"

"In England we'd call her eccentric. Sounds posher than odd somehow. The English love their eccentrics."

"Well," she says, "the English have never met Mama Dean."

Charlie laughs again. "She sounds like my mum. Whenever anyone does anything odd, we call it 'doing a Nellie.' That was Mum's name, Nellie. Only it wasn't pickles with her, it was concoctions of vinegar and honey, God save us. She thought it would cure anything."

Betty laughs and suddenly her shoulders relax and the knot in her stomach eases. "Thanks for telling me about your mother," she says. "And thanks for inviting me to Annie's party. I'm not sure how I'll do it, but I'll try my best to be there."

When she catches her reflection in the bathroom mirror it surprises her. She hasn't looked this happy in a long time.

JULY 1985

11

Jill

....

Right after her mother left, a few people came to the house with casseroles and cakes. But they didn't sit around the front room looking sad, the way they did after a funeral. Instead they said a few awkward words, shoved a dish in Jill's direction, and before she could think of anything to say, they got in their cars and drove off.

Of course, even if they had waited for her to say something, for the first few days, all she had managed was, "No shit!"

That's what she'd said when her father called them at Grandmother Presson's house that weekend. She remembers Amy answered the phone; that she'd grabbed the edge of Grandmother's antique desk and started to cry.

She remembers her first thought was that something had happened to Mama Dean. "Amy?" she'd mumbled through stiff lips. "What's wrong?"

"It's Mama. Mama left."

"Mama?" she'd said, to be sure she'd heard it right. "Mama left?"

"Daddy says they had a fight and she left. That was two nights ago!"

She'd grabbed the phone from her sister and made her father repeat what had happened. When he was finished, she'd said, "No shit."

And even though she'd said it in stunned disbelief, she knew in her heart it was true. Because, for the first time in her life, her father hadn't scolded her for cussing.

After she got back home, she'd open a closet door, and notice the empty spaces where her mother's jacket and sweater had hung, and she'd said, "No shit!"

She'd said it again when she'd opened a cupboard door and realized that her mother's coffee mug hadn't been moved all day. Again, when she'd noticed that the foyer rug looked bare, then remembered that was where her mother always kicked off her sneakers.

At night when she couldn't sleep she'd whispered, "If Mama comes home, I'll be nice to her from now on. I won't fight with Daddy. I'll keep my room clean. I won't threaten to run away. I won't get any more tattoos."

She knew she was making a deal with God, even though in tenth grade she'd had a fight with her father and told him she didn't believe in God. She remembers her mother's stricken face, how the veins in her father's neck stood out as he'd stomped out of her room in a huff.

She'd known she'd gone too far when she'd said it, but she'd wanted to hurt him. She'd have said anything to make him leave her alone.

When she'd heard the car pull out of the driveway, them going off to church without her, she remembers lying in bed under her comforter, thinking she'd won.

But, after that, the fights got worse. After that, she and Daddy fought about everything all the time. Then Mama and Daddy would argue and Daddy would slam into his den. Sometimes he wouldn't speak to any of them for days. When that happened, Mama would tell them everything was all right, but she gnawed her lip and jumped at the least little sound when she'd said it.

Maybe everything that happened was her fault. Maybe her mother left because she was sick to death of fighting with Daddy trying to defend her. Maybe if she hadn't always had to have the last word, always had to go too far, her family would be together and happy right now.

She'd added that to her list. "If Mama comes home, I promise I won't be a complete bitch anymore."

That was weeks ago and she'd lived up to her part of the bargain. She'd stopped fighting with her father. She'd kept the house clean. She'd stopped going out with her friends. She'd stopped fighting with Amy. She'd even stopped her wood carving, the one thing she was good at, the thing that meant everything to her.

For weeks she'd done all these things. But no matter what she did nothing seemed to change. Her mother still hadn't come home. Her father still stayed locked up in his den.

This afternoon when their mother had cornered them in the parking lot at Dixie Burger, then forced them to go to her stupid apartment—didn't she know that was the last place they wanted to be? It was bad enough that she'd moved out and had a place of her own. Why did she have to rub their noses in it by taking them there?

Today she hadn't even looked like their mother. She'd worn snug jeans and a punked-up hairdo like Tina Turner's, as if she thought of herself as a cool older sister, not their mother at all.

Even now when Jill thought about it she got so pissed off she wanted to trash something, burn something, drive down East Main Street at a hundred miles an hour.

It had shocked her that Amy had been the one who ran out of the apartment. Amy had always been Miss Priss, Miss Perfect, the twin who always did the "right thing." Amy always dressed like a page out of *Seventeen*. While she, the evil twin, had an eagle tattooed on her butt and dressed like Pocahontas. Why, Amy got a scholarship to the University at Chapel Hill, the same day Jill had been expelled for helping to carry the vice principal's Volkswagen into the school lobby.

But now, Amy was at the mall with her stuck-up friends, pretending that the scene at their mother's apartment never happened.

Her father wasn't at home tonight either. He was probably at one of his dumb-ass meetings.

Only she, the wild child, the twin who always went too far, was wandering through the big, empty house wondering why God hadn't lived up to His end of the bargain.

She went outside and crossed the yard to the garage workshop. She ducked inside, locked the door behind her, and came face-to-face with a cigar store Indian. Propped against the wall, next to him, was a six-foot-tall totem pole.

The other three walls are covered from floor to ceiling with makeshift shelves. The top shelves are jam-packed with carvings of small animals: squirrels, rabbits, foxes. Other shelves are loaded with carvings of birds, everything from hummingbirds to doves to fierce-eyed eagles. The bottom shelves hold life-size carvings of heads: Indian women, braves, chiefs, and children.

The medicine woman, Jill's favorite carving, is in the center of the workbench. Next to it is a basket filled to the brim with adobe houses the size of her fist. The adobe houses are her moneymakers. She can whittle a few after supper, then carry a duffel bag full to the flea market, and sell them for five dollars apiece.

She's saved over a hundred dollars, hoping against hope that Chief Too-Tall, a local master carver, will agree to take her on as a student.

For two years, she'd dragged branches, sometimes whole dead trees home to the workshop. She'd carved for hours, behind locked doors, only stopping when her belly grumbled or her father shouted, "For God sake, Jill, turn off that damned chainsaw!"

She takes a deep breath, inhaling the scent of fresh-cut wood, then pats the medicine woman. She remembers how excited she'd been the first time she'd imagined this carving, how she stayed awake nights planning every detail; then she'd held her breath as she started the painstaking work. There were times she got so lost in the work that hours felt like minutes. Sometimes when her father called she was so caught up in what she was doing she honestly didn't hear him.

But now, a few weeks later, she stares at the medicine woman, at the chisel and adz collecting dust on the workbench, and shrugs, waiting to feel something.

When that doesn't happen, she goes back to her room, climbs out on the roof, and lights a joint.

12

Betty

....

Dear Annie,

I'm sorry I couldn't talk when you called the other night. The minute I got on the phone, Mama Dean came out to the kitchen and stood there, two feet away from me. She didn't say the first word, didn't even look at me. She just stood there, the whole time we were talking, pretending to stare out the window.

She doesn't have the first clue about a person needing a little privacy. So, if I sounded funny, that's why. All I could do was talk about the weather and that recipe for Celestial Golden Salad, and say over and over again, "I'm fine. Just fine."

The truth is, I think I'm having a midlife crisis at the age of fifty-six. Used to, I thought that was people's excuse for sports cars, face-lifts, and messing around. But suddenly I'm not sure what's right or wrong, what's brave or foolish or if what I've believed in was ever really true.

Maggie was here last week. It was the first time we'd had a real talk since she left home. She'd had a fight with her girls and for a minute all

I wanted to do was shake her, but then I realized she was already torn up. When she finally settled down, we talked. We said a lot of things that had needed to be said for a long time. Then, she brought up her daddy and me—how leaving a husband seemed to run in the family—and it flew all over me. Here I was, letting my guard down, trying to be close to her again, and she'd turned on me for no reason.

But now I've spent all week thinking about what she said. And I realize how it must have seemed to her. I did leave her daddy. And even though I'd had a lot of good reasons, he was still her daddy. I never explained. Wouldn't even talk about it. I just expected her to accept it as a fact of her life.

Now, she was saying, I need you to take my word for it, to accept my decision. Oh, Annie, why couldn't I see it before? I've been so hard on her when I'd done the same thing. But all I could see was that Steven was settled and respectable—everything I'd ever wanted for her.

Do you remember when I left Jack? I felt like I'd come home to Poplar Grove in disgrace. Jack drank too much and changed jobs too often, but I was too ashamed to tell anyone. I didn't try to explain or defend myself. I just let people think what they wanted and tried to live through the gossip the best way I could. I kept my head down and made up my mind to work the swing shift for the rest of my life, if I had to, to do whatever it took to give Maggie a decent life.

By the time Maggie was in high school I thought things were going to turn out all right, but that boy, Jerry Roberts, started coming around. Maggie was crazy about him and it scared me to death. I thought he was wild. I was afraid if I didn't do something drastic she'd wind up just like me. So the minute she graduated I sent her off to live with her daddy.

Then she met Steven and I remember thinking, thank goodness. Now she has a chance—a chance for a safe, happy life. But one day, without a word to anyone, she took this great life—this safe, respectable life—and threw it away with both hands. I was shocked. I couldn't have been more upset if she'd told me she was shooting up heroin. I worried about what would happen to her and the girls—worried about what people would say. I wanted her to explain, to justify what she'd done.

All those years I'd thought that if I was a good, decent woman, that if I worried enough, sacrificed enough, everything would turn out right. So when she said leaving a husband ran in the family, I thought she was sneering at everything I'd tried to do for her.

Now that I know what she was really trying to say, I've been thinking about my life, thinking about it, and questioning everything.

Oh, Annie, sometimes I walk the halls of the Alzheimer's Unit and I wonder if they spent their whole lives keeping their heads down, trying to do the right thing. Did they tell themselves that if they tried hard enough everything would work out? What would they do different if they had the chance to do it over again? A few of them are only in their fifties. I can't help but wonder if I'm about to run slam out of chances.

I'm sorry to write such a depressing letter. You probably wish you'd never offered me a shoulder to cry on.

Love,

Betty

P.S. The Celestial Golden Salad calls for oranges, but it's mandarin oranges, not the regular kind. They come in cans—2 for 89 cents at the

Winn-Dixie. Also, be sure to use frozen orange juice. *I used regular once and it just wouldn't jell.*

P.S. #2 I'm thinking about coloring my hair. What do you think about auburn or a nice chestnut brown?

P.S. #3 The old Hatley house, next door, has been sold. Word around town is they're going to level it and put up a Texaco gas station. Mama Dean's going to have a pure fit the way they're tearing up Jake!

The minute Betty mails the letter she worries that she'd sounded full of self-pity, that she's turning into one of those women who play poker with Mama Dean on Fridays—Gladys Spivey, Geneva Whitlock—whining, complaining women who talk about nothing but family feuds, ungrateful children, and the world going to hell in a handbasket. Why, the only time they smile and nod with satisfaction is when one of them says, "Law me, it's the Bible fulfilling itself. The end of the world is coming."

Betty has always avoided these women like a virus. Now, Annie will think she's one of them.

She's been working on the yard since dawn. At noon she'll call Annie—tell her to ignore the letter—say that she was a mess that day and everything's all right now.

The ancient mower shudders as she pushes it into the garden's high weeds. She forces the rusty lever into low gear, slows her pace, feels the perspiration trickle between her breasts. The motor shudders again, nearly dies, then makes a sound like it has bronchitis. Sweat blurs her eyes. She wipes her brow with her forearm, feels her bermuda shorts stick to her thighs. She waits, wondering if the mower will give out first or if she will. She has babied it all morning, mowing for a while, then letting it rest, while she pulled weeds by hand, attacked unruly bushes with clippers, battered stubborn garden stalks flat to the ground when the sling blade was too dull to cut them. Now she's too tired to coax the mower along. All she wants to do is finish. The lawn, which will never be smooth and even, is at least neat and tidy. Trash bags crowd the curb. This fall, when the weather is cooler, she'll do away with the garden. Dig it up. Plow it under. Plant it with grass. Pave it with concrete if she has to.

She couldn't care less. Nobody cares if her green bean casserole comes fresh from the garden or straight from the can.

Betty checks her watch. Eleven forty-five. In fifteen minutes she'll call Annie.

The mower coughs, then makes an anemic wheezing sound. They press on, finishing another slow row before it sputters and dies. But, this time, after ten minutes of trying to resuscitate it, there are no vital signs. She sighs, pats the mower's rusty head, then guides it to its final resting place at the curb with the trash bags.

Then she wipes her hands on her shorts legs, goes into the house, and picks up the phone.

Annie's alto voice says, "Hey."

Suddenly Betty's strength leaves her and she feels tongue-tied. "Hey, it's me, Betty."

"Betty! You doing all right, hon?"

"Doing fine. Did you get my letter?"

"Got it today. Is everything all right?"

Betty touches her eyes. "Well, I called to tell you, I'm a mess and I'm sorry. Sorry about the letter. Sorry that all I do is whine and complain."

"Well, forever more. With all you've got on you, it's a wonder you're not crazy as a bessie-bug."

Betty laughs. She hasn't heard "bessie-bug" for years and the words tickle her. "Well, I just didn't want to worry you."

"You always say that. I don't know why you worry about it. I thought that's what life was about. Figuring things out, griping to your friends. You know what your real problem is?"

Betty thinks about Maggie, Mama Dean, her granddaughters, her job, Fayette Chupp, the house falling to rack and ruin. She sighs. "Sad to say, but I do."

"You need to stare at water."

"What?"

"You need to stare at water. And I don't mean the bathtub kind neither. You've been on overload too long. You need to come for a visit, to stare at the ocean until your mind runs clear."

Betty closes her eyes. She can almost feel the sun on her skin. She imagines the roar of the ocean, seagulls and transistor radios murmuring in the background, soft breezes tangy with salt water and Coppertone.

She's on the verge of accepting Annie's invitation when she remembers the surprise party is only two weeks away. What if Charlie Love and the Brunch Bunch plan to have the party at Annie's place? Maybe they'd already arranged to keep her busy and distracted away from the double-wide that day while they got things set up. If she stayed with Annie that weekend could she keep Annie busy and distracted, or would her being there just be one more complication? Maybe she should call Charlie Love before she tells Annie she's coming.

"Betty? Are you still there?

"Sorry. I was just thinking . . . uh . . . would you mind if I call you back?"

"Is everything all right?"

"Everything's fine. I just thought of something I need to take care of right away. But I swear, I'll call you right back."

She hangs up, takes a deep breath, and dials again. "Hello, Charlie, this is Betty. I need to ask you a question."

For weeks Betty had thought it would take an act of Congress to get her to the beach the weekend of Annie's party, but suddenly things started falling into place. When she'd talked to Charlie he'd said, "That's wonderful news, love. You'll be the perfect distraction for Annie and I can't wait to meet you." Later that same day, Dot Skurlock remembered that when her daughter needed an emergency cesarean last spring, Betty covered for her. Now Dot returns the favor by signing up to work Betty's four-day weekend.

A few days later, she's wandering through the aisles at the flea market, hoping to find a gift for Annie, when she hears, "Hey, Grandy, what are you doing here?"

It's Jill. She's dressed like Sacajewea and standing near a display of wood carvings. Betty thinks she looks thin and tired. "Well, sugar, what are *you* doing here?" Betty says, hugging her granddaughter tight.

"This is my booth," Jill says proudly.

"Well, if that doesn't beat all. Seventeen years old and you're not only an artist, you're an entrepreneur. How long have you been coming here?"

"About a year, off and on."

Betty shakes her head, "Lordhavemercy. Well, I guess I do need to get out of the house more often."

"Don't worry about it. I don't talk about it much."

"Why not?"

Jill ducks her head. "Some people don't get it and I don't need the hassle."

"Well, I think it's wonderful. Maybe you can help me. I'm looking for a present . . . " Betty finds herself rattling on and on about Annie's party, Dot Skurlock's offer to work in her place and how, now, the only fly in the cocoa butter is to figure out what to do with Mama Dean. Suddenly her voice trails off. Among the row of bird carvings she's spotted the perfect gift for Annie.

"Oh, Jill," she says, "those sandpipers are beautiful. How did you get their little legs so slanty? They look like they're really darting along the beach."

"Gosh, Grandy. I'm glad you like 'em."

"Like them. I love them. They'd be the very thing for my friend."

"Oh, Grandy, I won't sell them to you."

"What do you mean?"

"I can't sell them to my own grandmother. But if you really want them, I'll give them to you."

"Oh, no, you won't," Betty says. "Today I'm not your grandmother. Today I'm just a regular paying customer. Did you eat yet, honey?"

Jill shakes her head and laughs. "Yeah, right. Of course you're just a regular customer. *All* my paying customers ask me if I ate yet."

While her granddaughter wraps the sandpipers in tissue paper, Betty wanders to the food court. She returns a few minutes later carrying Cokes and foot-long hot dogs and hands one of each to Jill. "So, what have you and your sister been up to?"

A moment before Jill had been lit up like Christmas, but now she looks depressed. "Nothing much. Amy and Daddy are never at home." Then she shrugs. "But, that's all right. It gives me a chance to hang out, you know, and work on my carvings."

"Well, you tell Amy I want you both to come to supper before you go off to school. And if she can't make it, you come yourself."

"Thanks. I don't know what Amy's up to, but I'm not doing anything tonight. Oh, and Grandy, when you go off on your beach trip, don't worry about Mama Dean. I'll come over and stay with her."

Two hours later, Betty is in the kitchen boiling potatoes for potato salad when Jill appears at the back door dragging her duffle and sleeping bag behind her. She lets herself in then walks past Betty, avoiding her eyes.

Betty is confused. She wipes her hands on a dish towel and follows her granddaughter down the hall. But when she gets to Maggie's old bedroom, Jill is staring out the window with her back to the door. "Jill," she says, "I'm not sure if I told you, but I won't be going to the beach 'til next weekend?"

"That's all right," Jill says. "I thought I'd stay for a while, have a real visit, you know, before I go off to school and all . . . "

It isn't until Betty hears the snag in her voice that she realizes Jill's been crying. She aches to hug her. There are a thousand things she wants to ask. Are you missing your mother? Do you need someone to talk to? But Jill stays facing the window, making it clear that she doesn't want hugs or questions. She doesn't want anyone, not even her grandmother, to know she's been crying.

"Well, then, sugar," Betty says, quietly backing out of the room. "You just go ahead and get settled while I finish fixing supper."

On Friday morning, Betty carries her suitcase to the car. But she still won't believe she's actually leaving until she's on Route 73.

She's already driven through China Grove, Concord, and Albemarle before she realizes that her shoulders are hunched somewhere in the vicinity of her ears. She lowers them. But by now her neck is so tight that every time she moves her head it makes crackling sounds like bubble wrap. Traffic is heavy as she merges onto Route 74 at Rockingham and she feels her neck tighten again. At Laurinburg the traffic thins out and she stops at Wendy's for lunch. But this time when she studies the map she feels lighter, as if a weight has been lifted from her. It's really happening. She's halfway to the beach!

At Whiteville, thirty-five miles from Annie's, she pulls into a McDonald's. Her reflection in the rest-room mirror startles her. She has forgotten about her new hairdo. Maggie had colored and styled it this morning before the shop opened. But with packing and driving she hasn't had a chance to get used to it.

Mama Dean had taken one look at her, and said, "Law me, you look like your hair's been boiled and hung upside down to dry."

But Jill had followed her to the car and said, "Don't worry about her. I love Mama Dean to death, but she's living in the dark ages. If she had her way you'd wear nothing but tight perms, blue rinses, and double knit. You look kicking, Grandy."

Betty still wasn't sure what "kicking" meant, but it had to beat "boiled and hung upside down to dry."

Now she pats her moussed chestnut curls and thinks about Annie, meeting the Brunch Bunch and Charlie Love. For a second she panics. Then she takes a deep breath and walks to the pay phone in the parking lot.

"Annie, it's me. I'll be there in forty-five minutes."

"Well, come on, girlfriend." Annie's voice is a wonderful rising welcome. "The sun tea's ready and Patsy Cline's on the boom box."

13

Betty

....

Right after supper, Betty and Annie load folding chairs and a cooler into the car then drive the three miles to the beach. They pass a strip mall, a makeshift stand with a BOILED PEANUTS sign, several peeling pink and turquoise trailers in tiny weed-choked yards; then a red-faced, fat man, shirtless and wearing bib overalls, is selling shrimp from the back of an old pickup. When they reach the top of the Ocean Isle Bridge and Betty sees the limitless expanse of ocean, the contrast is so startling, she gasps.

"I know," Annie, says, quietly. "Every time I drive over this bridge I have to have a moment of silence. Even after all these years it still feels like a religious experience."

They drive on past a combination gas station, motel, and real estate office, a few spindly palm trees, a huge fiberglass giraffe, then a waterslide surrounded by chain-link fencing. Annie parks the car behind a cement-block building, spray-painted with the words GRILL—GAMES—LIVE BAIT.

They get out of the car, cross the blacktop parking lot, then start up the wooden stairs to the beach.

When they get to the landing, Annie pauses and points toward the horizon. "Last summer, I was standing right here with some of the Brunch Bunch when there was a total eclipse of the moon. I tell you, it was so amazing, I almost expected to hear a celestial choir."

Betty stares out at the ocean, trying to take it all in, but she still hasn't got her bearings. Her beach chair bangs against her shins and she switches her canvas tote from one slippery Coppertoned shoulder to the other, as she follows Annie's flip-flops down the steps, then across the sand. She isn't at home with Annie yet, either. It's only been three years since they've seen each other. But that friend was plump, gray, and motherly. The friend she met today is trim, has a strawberry-blond pixie hairdo, and calls her outfit a "romper."

They've gone a good fifty yards down the beach when Annie stops so suddenly Betty nearly runs into her. "This is it! My spot. Funny how certain spots feel right, like they belong to you. We'll set up our beach chairs, and walk off our supper if you're not too tired from your trip."

Betty nods and they kick off their shoes, then cross the wet, packed sand to the water's edge.

A few minutes before, the beach had been dotted with umbrellas and folding chairs, blankets, and playpens, but most of the people have left without Betty noticing.

Now the beach seems to belong to the walkers. There are a few families. A father with a kite string cuts in front of them, followed by two small, squealing children. But the others are mostly in pairs: a woman with a look-alike teenage daughter, young couples, old couples, some holding hands.

Betty wonders how long it's been since she's held anyone's hand. "Do you think you'll ever marry again?" she asks.

Annie sighs. "I don't know. The last guy I dated was one of those, 'When I want your opinion, I'll give it to you' kinds."

Betty eyes go big as something that's been tugging at her mind eases and falls into place. "I've met that kind. Now that I think about it, Maggie's Steven was probably that kind."

Annie squints into the sun. "Bless her heart. But what about you? Do you think you'll ever marry?"

"Used to, I thought I would. If I met the right person. But so far the men in Poplar Grove haven't amounted to much."

Annie laughs. "You've been single and living in Poplar Grove for over thirty years. No offense, Betty, but that's a mighty long time to still be calling it 'so far.'"

"What can I say? Pickings are slim in Poplar Grove. The good ones are taken and the rest are roosters."

"Roosters?"

"You know. Like that old song, 'A Good-Hearted Woman in Love with a Good-Timing Man.' You know, those rascals who run around, drinking up the paycheck, while the sweet little wife stays home with the baby, keeping supper warm and avoiding the landlord."

Annie laughs. "I'll swan! You always could paint a picture. But they can't all be roosters."

"The ones I met were. Besides, I'd already had all that mess with Jack and I had a child to raise."

"But Maggie's been raised a long time."

"I know. But even when I was twenty, they weren't exactly beating down my door. By the time she was raised they'd stopped asking. It's been a year now since anyone asked me to go anywhere."

Annie's eyes widen. "What was he like?"

"His idea of a date was to ask me to help him hoe his garden! He was actually shocked when I didn't jump at the chance."

They laugh and walk on, side by side, brushing shoulders, then moving apart.

"Oh, honey, that's the trouble," Annie says. "Plenty of women would jump at the chance. Why, they come in droves, carrying casseroles to widowers whose wives aren't even in the ground yet."

"All he has to be is single and breathing."

"I know," Annie says. "Still, it does get lonesome."

Suddenly a wave hits them, soaking their shorts. They squeal like children, then pick up their feet and wade closer to shore.

Annie tugs at her sun visor. "What kind of man do you want?"

"Oh, someone who's understanding. Intelligent. Sensitive. Someone I can talk to." Suddenly Charlie Love floats into her mind and she shakes her head to clear it.

"What about a sense of humor? I can't abide a man without a sense of humor."

Betty nods. Here we are, she thinks. Two middle-aged women still trying to understand the strange behavior of men, but still trotting out our perfect-man list, just like we did back in school.

"You're right," she says. "He's definitely got to have a sense of humor."

"And it wouldn't hurt if he looked like Robert Redford, right?"

"I don't care that much about looks."

Annie frowns. "Yeah, but what if he has all the qualities you want, but he's just a little gnome of a man? What if he looks like Aristotle Onassis or something?"

Betty laughs again. She can't remember the last time she laughed this much. "Lord, Annie, you always were a mess. But what about you? What kind of man do you want?"

For a moment Annie is so quiet, Betty wonders if she's heard. Finally, she says, "The same as you. I just want someone who'll know what I'm worth."

They stare out toward the ocean, letting their gaze rest on the shimmering water. Betty wonders where the waves have been—had they formed somewhere in the middle of the ocean? Or had they started on the opposite shore, the other side of the world? What country was on the opposite shore, anyway? England? Spain? Africa, maybe? She sighs. She's always longed to travel, but her geography is hopelessly muddled. Betty has her own theories about the world and its workings. She likes her theories better than actual facts. Her favorite is the one about high tides and low tides. At low tide, someone, probably the man in the moon, pulls a plug. Then, when the water starts getting too low, he just turns on a huge faucet and fills up the ocean's bathtub.

They walk on, passing hotels, condominiums, and rental cottages. They pick their way around sand tunnels and castles and forgotten beach toys. Annie grabs Betty's arm just in time to save her from stepping on a dead jellyfish. They both shriek and walk the next twenty yards or so watching their feet.

A few minutes later, Annie raises her sun visor, then stops. "The sun is starting to set. We probably need to get back. We can come back again tomorrow afternoon."

They stand and stare at the horizon as the egg-yolk sun slips into the ocean. Betty almost expects to hear the water sizzle, then come to a rolling boil.

She thinks about tomorrow and the logistics for Annie's party. Charlie Love has insisted they come to his cottage for a before-dinner birthday drink. But Annie would never forgive her if they showed up sticky and sand-covered from the beach, Annie expecting a casual drink then ending up being the center of attention at her own surprise party. They'd have to walk the beach in the morning. Then she'd tell Annie to spruce up—she's taking her out to lunch for her birthday. They'd take their time, maybe do a little souvenir shopping, and arrive at the cottage in their casual best.

She takes a deep breath. It is hard to believe that tomorrow she'll finally meet her mysterious English caller.

By the time they spot their green-and-white beach chairs, the sky has gone from peach to crimson, faded denim to purple. Now, a fingernail moon lights their way down the wooden steps to the parking lot.

They have just driven over the Ocean Isle Bridge, heading west, when Annie says, quietly, "I've been wanting to tell you . . . I've met someone."

Betty blinks. "Oh, Annie, that's great."

"Yeah," Annie says. "It's the oddest thing. I didn't really just meet him. He's someone I've known for a while, someone who's been under my nose all along."

"Is it someone from Raleigh?"

In the dark, Annie's voice sounds faraway dreamy. "No. It's better than that. He lives right here. He's one of the men in the Brunch Bunch."

14

Mama Dean

....

Mama Dean has been calling the Curl & Swirl all morning. She's trying to reach Maggie. But when anyone else answers the phone, she doesn't ask for Maggie, or say anything at all, she just hangs up. She knows what kind of rigmarole goes on at the Curl & Swirl. How they love to gossip. Well, they can gossip about someone else. It isn't anybody's business who she calls and she's not about to give them the satisfaction of knowing it's her.

Still, it is just like Maggie not to be there when she wants to tell her a thing or two.

She flips the TV to the Home Shopping Channel, turns off the sound, and dials again. Maybe this time, the voice on the other end will be her granddaughter's.

Finally, somewhere in the vicinity of the fifth or sixth call, Maggie answers. But, by then, Mama Dean can't think of a single thing to say. She lets the static crackle over the line and hangs up without a word. Still, it's a relief to know that Maggie is there. What with all that's happened it wouldn't surprise her if the girl had run off to Kalamazoo.

She sighs, leans back in her chair, and rocks awhile. "Law me," she mutters. "All this mess has tied a knot in my last nerve."

It just wasn't right. Maggie had left her family and was working at the Curl & Swirl, Betty was lollygagging on a beach somewhere, leaving her to deal with Jill. And it seemed to her that Jill was up to no good, too. Why, she was either sulking in her room, running up the electric bill with that chainsaw of hers, or going off with her long-haired friends.

Why, only this morning she had gone to the flea market with a bunch of them. Odd-looking girls. Scraggily-haired boys in sloppy, baggy clothes.

They'd all been sitting at the kitchen table, drinking iced tea, when she'd walked into the room. "Jill," she'd said. "Them boys is hippies."

Everyone got real quiet and Jill just stared at her. "They are not," she'd said.

"They are too. Why, two of them is wearing head scarves."

The girls all laughed. But they weren't any better than the boys. One of them was named Freedom. At first she thought the girl had said Freda, but it was Freedom, sure enough. She had never, in all her life, heard any such. But, the beatingest thing was that the girl wore her hair as short as a death-row convict, and when she'd turned around, she had a T-niney ponytail. Bright red.

"Lordymercy, child. How did you come to have such a bright red ponytail?"

Jill had acted all embarrassed, but the girl, this Freedom girl, just laughed. "Oh, Jill, your great-grandmother's a trip!" Then, she'd turned to Mama Dean and said, "Kool-Aid. I dyed it with cherry-berry Kool-Aid. Cool, huh?"

Before she left, Jill said something about the girl's parents teaching at some college in Charlotte. But she wasn't the least impressed. They might have fine la-di-dah educations, but calling their child Freedom and letting her dye her hair with red Kool-Aid . . . well, there had to be a hippie in the woodpile somewhere.

Hippies mean trouble. And if there's one thing she knows, it's how to spot trouble. It wears her out just thinking about it. That's why she let it drop—let Jill go on to the flea market with them. She just didn't have the energy to get into it with her.

She'd spotted trouble with Maggie, too. Seen it coming a mile away. But nobody would listen to her. For months Maggie had been acting right peculiar. Mooning around the house. Crying over nothing. Betty said that Maggie was going through a hard time. But what did that child know about hard times? The Depression was hard times. Watching men go off to war was hard times. Having a husband desert you and you with a child to raise, then being laid-off at the shirt factory every little whipstitch—that was hard times.

Why, Maggie had a fine house in the historical part of town, a husband, and a family. It was true Mama Dean herself wanted to pinch Steven's head off from time to time. Sometimes he got awful bossy, like he thought he was better than any of them. But he was a good man and always worked steady. Why, he'd even given Maggie that add-a-pearl necklace.

Last spring, when the trouble first started, she'd reminded Maggie of that, hoping she'd count her blessings. But Maggie said, "Lord, Mama Dean. That was nineteen years ago. It's hard to parlay a nineteen-year-old add-a-pearl necklace into a reason for living."

Sometimes, she wanted to pinch Maggie's head off too.

Steven didn't drink or run around. And he'd never raised a hand to Maggie. Why, she'd have taken a hickory switch to him herself if he'd tried that. Maggie had to realize that nobody's life was perfect.

But Maggie just kept getting more and more peculiar. She'd even changed her hair from normal to one of those finger-in-a-socket styles. Next thing they knew she'd left home. And that was all they wrote.

Now, all she could do was pray that Maggie wouldn't turn out like her daddy, Smiling Jack, or her grandfather, Donley. Or, come to think about it, just about anyone in Donley's family. Why, Donley's baby sister, Willie Ruth, smoked on the streets, wore backless dresses, and dyed her hair shoe-polish black way back in the twenties. And travel! Lord, how that girl loved to travel . . . California, Florida, New Orleans . . . no telling where all. She never lit in one place for more than a year. She'd been married something like four or five times. It was hard to keep count since the ink was barely dry on one divorce decree before she took up with somebody else. For years, Willie Ruth had worried her to death. But Donley just laughed about it—said Willie Ruth was born with one foot in the wind. Then, one day, Willie Ruth hanged herself, in a hotel in Nashville. Nobody ever knew why. They never even talked about it. But, after that, Donley was never the same.

She stares out the window, rocks a little harder, and decides she can't think about that now. The past is over and done with and she's got too much on her mind now what with Maggie ruining her life, Betty off gallivanting, and Jill up to Lord knows what, with Lord knows who.

Why, as far back as she could remember, the entire family tree was loaded with peculiar, hard-headed people who couldn't be told, and it didn't look like that was going to change anytime soon.

She had worked hard all her life. Too hard. And worried. Lord, she liked to have worried herself to death. Well, maybe it was time for her to enjoy herself. Kick up her heels a little.

Tonight she's been invited to Ada Jennings's for supper. Last month, Ada had sold her house and moved to the Oaks Retirement Village. Everyone said the Oaks was real nice. Ada said that except for family, Mama Dean was the first person she'd invited. Ada even offered to come by and pick her up.

She stares out the window and rocks a little harder. She has a good mind to call Ada, tell her she'll be glad to come to supper. Why, the mood she is in, she might just pack her bags and *move* to the Oaks. It'd serve them right if she didn't so much as leave a note. For once let them wonder where she was and what she was up to.

15

Jill

....

"Oh, shit. I don't believe it," Jill tells Freedom as she spots her father and Theo Bloodworth browsing in the next booth at the flea market.

She ducks behind her display table, pulling Freedom in after her. "I don't want him to see me," she hisses. "Get up there! Pretend it's your booth."

Freedom stands up and looks around. "Who? What are you talking about?"

"It's my father! Don't look at me. You'll give me away!"

Freedom sighs. "All right. All right. What do you want me to do? I don't even know what he looks like."

"A yuppie."

"That's a big help," Freedom says sarcastically. "The place is crawling with yuppies."

"Blond hair. Blue Izod shirt. Khakis."

"All right. All right. I think I see him. Is he with a woman who looks like old money?"

"Yes."

"That's him, then. Oh, God, he's looking this way."

"Don't look! Just tell me when the coast is clear," Jill says, crawling under the table.

When she hears feet shuffling toward her, she pulls the edge of the display cloth around herself like a tent. A moment later she sees the shadows of two pairs of legs, just inches from her face. She holds her breath and shifts her position, making herself as small as possible.

This is stupid, she thinks, hiding from her father, especially at a flea market, underneath a table of wood carvings. He'd recognize her work. And if he didn't, Mrs. Bloodworth would.

At her graduation party her mother had put the unfinished head of the medicine woman in the center of the table and Mrs. Bloodworth had made a big fuss over it. Then she insisted on seeing the rest of Jill's work. She'd called the carvings "powerful, primitive, almost primordial." Jill had never paid much attention to Mrs. Bloodworth before. She'd just thought of her as one of the people who went to *beaucoup* meetings with her father. She'd never thought of her as old money either. She wore clothes Jill had only seen in vintage consignment shops—suits edged in silk, cameo brooches. Once Jill's mother had said, "She even wears her hair in a chignon, like the late Princess Grace!" Whoever that was. But she *was* Dr. Bloodworth's widow and lived in that big house on West Main. And, that day, graduation day, Mrs. Bloodworth had talked on and on about Jill's talent, then she'd said, "Oh, Steven. You simply *must* send this child to art school." Jill's father smiled, then gathered everyone in the dining room to announce that he would send her to art school in the fall and Chief Too-Tall's summer classes.

Like an idiot, she'd believed him. But two weeks ago, long after her mother was gone, and Mrs. Bloodworth wasn't around to impress, he'd said, "No daughter of mine is taking classes with some Indian chief. I've signed you up for computer classes and that's all there is to that."

That's when she'd run off to stay with Grandy and Mama Dean. She'd told Amy where she'd be, but she hadn't so much as called her father. After what he'd done, she didn't intend to ever speak to him again.

Now, Freedom is saying, "Hey, you all. Can I help you?"

Jill holds her breath again. The concrete floor is cold and dusty and the space under the table is crowded with packing boxes and wadded-up newspaper.

A few minutes later, the feet move on.

"What's going on?" Jill whispers, but Freedom shushes her.

More feet shuffle toward her, then stop. Freedom says, "Feel free to browse. If you need any help, just ask."

Jill hears a woman's high-pitched voice say, "Y'all don't have any of those cute little garden gnomes, do you? Me and Mama just love garden gnomes, don't we, Mama?"

Jill pictures Freedom's shaved head, the bright-red ponytail, and longs to hear her say, "Honestly, ma'am. Do I look like someone who'd sell garden gnomes?"

Instead, Freedom says, "No, ma'am, I'm sorry."

Jill rolls her eyes. She'd rather take poison than make disgusting country cutesies. Still, at least a dozen people had asked for country geese, teddy bears, and now gnomes. She and Freedom hadn't made a dime all day. They just kept giving directions to Make Mine Country in building G.

Jill sighs. She needs to earn some money. Enough for a place of her own. Enough to pay for classes with Chief Too-Tall. She'd heard about artists paying their dues. Now she wonders if carving country cutesies is the price she'll have to pay.

16

Betty

....

All the way to Charlie's cottage, Annie talks about Sam Maddox, the man she is seeing, and the other members of the Brunch Bunch. Betty tries to concentrate, but Annie has stopped at every souvenir shop from Calabash to Shalotte and now they're running late.

When they finally pull into the driveway, Annie says, "Pretty, isn't it? Before he retired, Charlie had a landscaping business. He can make a yard look this good and still make it low maintenance."

Betty nods, as her eyes dart everywhere, searching for hidden cars and people. The cottage is a pretty Cape Cod in a soft pewter color with window boxes filled with pink geraniums, set on a half-acre lot.

As soon as the car comes to a complete stop, Betty opens her door to get out. But instead of hurrying, Annie is settling in, explaining, once again, why it is that Sam's out of town on her birthday. Then she takes her time in front of the rearview mirror, dabbing on fresh lipstick and fluffing her hair.

Betty takes a deep breath. She has promised to get Annie to the cottage and now they are here. No one can blame her if she can't pry Annie from the car. She tries to relax, considers checking her own hair and makeup. But someone, probably Charlie Love himself, is bound to be watching them from the window, calling out, "They're here," while everyone scrambles for a place to hide.

Just thinking about being watched makes Betty feel clumsy and self-conscious.

They get out of the car and walk up the driveway. They are just a few steps from the porch when Annie wanders over to the side yard to point out a shady rock garden filled with heather.

"See what I mean," she says. "Low maintenance."

Betty glances toward the house and sees a curtain move. "I think we should let him know we're here," she says.

"Wait, I want to show you something." Now, Annie is standing near a sunlit patch of wild flowers. "This is a butterfly garden," she says. "Sometimes this big purple bush is completely covered with Monarchs. Isn't that great?"

"Great," Betty mumbles.

Annie turns and looks at her. "Are you all right?"

"I feel like I'm trespassing. I don't even know this man and I'm walking all over his property."

"Oh, Charlie won't mind. Come on, there's a rose garden out back, I want you to see."

Betty glances toward the house and shrugs helplessly. A moment later, the door swings open and a man crosses the yard. He's wearing khaki shorts, a green knit shirt, and deck shoes. Despite his gray hair, his face is boyish. Betty recognizes Charlie Love from the photo of the Brunch Bunch taped to her refrigerator.

"Happy birthday, love," he says, giving Annie a hug. Then, "You must be Betty. I've heard so much about you," He smiles, looks into her eyes, and winks.

Then, all at once everything is a blur; Charlie is saying something about mad dogs and Englishmen out in the noonday sun; then a hand at her elbow guides her into a cool, dim room; soft music is playing in the background; and before she can get her bearings, people appear from everywhere, faces merge, voices call out, "Surprise! Happy Birthday!"

For a moment, Annie's face goes blank, then her chin quivers and she's laughing and crying at the same time.

"I can't believe this," she says. "No one's ever given me a party before."

A tall man with a neatly trimmed beard, dressed in navy shorts and a striped golf shirt, says, "Well, it's about time someone did, then." By the way he holds on to Annie, Betty decides he's Sam Maddox.

"Better late than never," a blond woman in a print sundress and gold sandals says.

A few people are laughing, while others ooh and aah.

Annie turns to Betty, "You were in on this, weren't you?"

Charlie grins. "We haven't been properly introduced, but these last few weeks Betty and I have become phone mates."

Annie looks at her, taking it all in. "So, that's why you've been twitchy all day!"

Betty laughs. "Who, me? Twitchy?"

"I was getting pretty twitchy myself," Charlie says. "If you'd made it to the rose garden, you'd have spotted the cars behind the shed."

Several people crowd in to hug Annie. As Betty steps aside, she backs into someone, and, once again, everything is a blur as she stumbles, scrambles to regain her footing, nearly rights herself, then feels herself falling.

Unseen hands reach out to steady her, holding her firmly until she regains her balance, then a voice murmurs softly, "Are you all right?" And suddenly Charlie Love is beside her, his face so close she can see the gold specks in his hazel eyes.

Betty has a wild impulse to reach out and touch his face, to smooth the soft hair at the nape of his neck. This feeling is so unexpected, so shocking, she puts her hands behind her back and holds them there stiffly for fear they'll take on a life of their own. This can't be happening. Not now. Not to her. She's fifty-six years old, a grandmother, a sensible, no-nonsense nurse. Feelings like this only happened to starry-eyed girls in romance novels.

Charlie is still holding on to her, his face filled with concern. "Are you sure you're all right?"

"I'm fine. Thanks. I just stumbled . . . lost my balance . . ."

Now he is saying something about far from the madding crowd as he leads her to the dining room. "Can I get you some iced tea? Maybe something stronger?"

"Tea would be nice. Thanks."

He pulls out a chair. "Sit down, won't you?"

Betty does what she's told, hoping to gather herself together.

There's a German chocolate birthday cake in the center of the table, surrounded by several small, framed photos—the photos she'd sent for Annie's birthday display. Annie alone. High school and nursing school photos of Annie and Betty together. Betty had forgotten about the photos. It is strange but comforting to see pictures of herself in a cottage she's never visited.

Charlie is moving toward the refrigerator, a trim compact man, wearing a shirt the same shade of green as his eyes. He gets two glasses from the cupboard, fills them with ice, then slices a lemon. Betty watches him intently—can't take her eyes off him. There's something thrilling, yet familiar, about watching this man putter around a kitchen.

He turns and looks at her. "Sweet?" he says.

Betty blinks. She's as startled as if she'd been watching a movie and the lead actor has asked her a question from the screen. "Yes," she says. "Betty Sweet."

For a moment Charlie looks confused, then he grins. "I mean, do you want your tea sweet or unsweetened?"

Betty's face feels hot. "Oh, Lord, I thought you meant . . . uh . . . sweet tea, thanks."

He's still smiling as he carries their glasses to the table. "I know what it's like," he says. "If you think Sweet's confusing, you ought to try going around with a name like Charlie Love. I've spent my life looking around every time someone says the word love. It's caused a few awkward moments, I can tell you."

They both laugh.

He sets the glasses on the table and extends his hand. "Hello, Betty Sweet. I'm Charlie Love. We sound like an old-fashioned song title, don't we?"

They both laugh again. And suddenly the panic is gone. Betty feels relaxed and happy, happier than she can ever remember. She has the strange sense of being at home, as if she has all the time in the world, as if anything is possible. She might not be a starry-eyed girl in a romance novel, but she knows something special has happened.

17

"Dammit, Maggie," Steven says. "I'd like to know what you're trying to pull this time?"

Maggie is shocked into silence. Steven's phone call is completely unexpected. He hasn't called once since they'd separated. Now, he's phoning her at work, and starting the conversation with "dammit." To make matters worse, it's Saturday and the shop is so busy they quit taking walk-ins at noon. There are women under dryers, women in curlers waiting for dryers, and several others, including Gladys Spivey, who are in the reception area just inches from the phone. Leave it to Steven to call, looking for a fight, when she's surrounded by a dozen bored, restless women, with nothing better to do than eavesdrop.

She considers taking the call in the break room, but she'd just put color on Ginger Catoe's roots and Ginger's eyes are darting from Maggie to the timer, and back again, for fear she'll be forgotten.

Maggie turns her back to the room and keeps her voice low. "I don't know what you're talking about."

"I'm talking about your daughter. You do remember your

daughter, don't you? The one who took off a week ago, without so much as a phone call?"

"You mean Jill?" she says.

"Very good, Maggie. You do remember her then?"

She feels the heat rise up her neck. "What do you want?"

Suddenly, the shop seems unnaturally quiet. Maggie looks around. When she'd answered the phone, the reception area was humming with conversation; now all the customers are engrossed in magazines. She takes a deep breath and pulls herself together.

"I want to know if she's staying with you, since you're both so determined to humiliate me."

She longs to say, "Are you paranoid? Have you lost your simple mind?" But Shirley, who is sweeping her section, raises her eyebrows then tilts her head warningly toward Gladys Spivey.

"Nope. I haven't seen her."

"Well, for your information, it took a lot of pull to get her into that computer school and now they're saying she never showed up."

Something in her mind clicks into place. Before she left for the beach, her mother said that Jill had suddenly turned up, crying, asking if she could stay, and she'd been brooding around the house ever since.

"So," she says quietly. "She took off the day you broke your promise about art school and signed her up for computer school. Is that what you're saying?"

Static crackles over the line. When Steven finally speaks, his voice is colder than she's ever heard it. "You're a fine one to talk about promises."

"Yeah, well, I might not be mother of the year, but it didn't take me a week to start looking for her. I guess that's why I know where she is and you don't."

Then, she hangs up the phone, just as Ginger's timer goes off.

"I guess I'll have to start stalking my own daughters," Maggie says, covering herself with the sheet.

Jerry props himself on one elbow. "You don't have to do that. They *are* your daughters."

"Think about it, Jerry. I can't just go talk to them. Amy's with Steven. Jill's at Mama Dean's."

His eyes widen. "Yeah. But stalking, I don't know, Maggie."

"Well, it wouldn't be stalking. Not really. I'd just drive past the house until Steven or Mama Dean go somewhere and the girls are alone. Or I could follow them to Dixie Burger or the flea market . . . you know . . . wherever."

"Come on, honey," he says, quietly.

She stares straight ahead. "I know. But after all they've been through, I need to keep an eye on them. Make sure they're all right. It'd be more like . . . uh . . . following."

He leans into her. "Okay. Following. Some people like being followed. Me, for instance. I love being followed. I'd love it if you followed me everywhere. But teenagers are funny about stuff like that."

Maggie moves to the side of the bed and sits up, taking the sheet with her. "Oh, Lord!" she moans. "I'm turning into Mama Dean! Remember how she followed us back in school. Listening in on my phone calls, reading my diary. She even got our schoolteacher boarders to spy on me. I hated it."

He reaches for her. "Hey, you, come back here. You're not like that. You're nothing like Mama Dean."

She lies down beside him, resting her head on his chest. "I hope not. But you're right. Even if I did track them down that doesn't mean they'd talk to me. And even if we talked, it's not like I have anything to offer them."

He kisses her hair. "We'll think of something. I'm pretty good in a crisis."

"Good thing. We've had nothing but crisis since we got together."

Jerry rolls onto his back and stares at the ceiling. "God, Maggie. I'm doing my best. We knew it'd be a mess for a while."

Maggie is stricken. "Not you. I didn't mean you," she says, leaning over him and kissing his hairline, his eyelids, his chin, then all the places in between. "Oh, honey, you're not a mess. You're great. It's me. I'm the mess. I come here every night with all my problems. I'm just one big walking, talking crisis."

"Oh, you're not that big," he says, smiling. "And I want you here every night, no matter how you come. Besides, some things are getting better."

"Like what?"

"Well, you went to see your mother."

"I did, didn't I."

"Yep. So things are better there. And you stood up to Steven."

"He was so hateful, blessing me out before I even knew who it was much less what he was talking about. I swear, he's more upset about looking bad at that computer school than he is that Jill's missing."

"Well, you really let him have it. You were great."

Maggie smiles. "I was kind of proud of myself. I would have said more, but then I remembered Gladys Spivey, sitting right there, listening in on everything."

"To hell with Gladys Spivey."

Maggie gasps, then laughs, at the unexpectedness of his words. "Jerry!"

"I mean it," he says. "You've spent your whole life tying to please small-minded people like her. But there's no pleasing them. I had to go away, join the Navy to figure that out. I mean, who's Gladys Spivey anyway? She can't kill us. She can't even send us to Vietnam. Why should we care what she thinks?"

Maggie laughs again. "I never thought of it like that."

They lie there quietly, listening to the crickets chirp and watching the light change from gold to pink then peach as the setting sun filters through the bedroom curtains. Finally Maggie says, "When I was little, Daddy used to call me fiesty—his fiesty little brown-haired girl. No one's called me that for a long time. But you know what?"

"What?"

"I think that feisty girl's still inside me somewhere. I just need to let her out more often."

18

Betty

. . . .

Betty lies in bed as the morning sun peeks through the slats in the mauve miniblinds in Annie's guest room. She had wakened several times during the night, not sure of where she was, wondering if she's been dreaming. Maybe she never really left home, never walked on the beach with Annie, and if meeting Charlie Love was only a dream, all she wants to do is go on sleeping.

She looks at the clock. Seven-thirty. The latest she's slept in years. Still, she lies there, taking in the room, trying to get her bearings. She sees the flowing print dress draped over a chair, the new beige sandals in a pigeon-toed heap nearby, but it isn't until she hears Annie stirring around in the next room that she finally begins to believe she hasn't been dreaming after all. Maybe her life really has taken a turn.

She slips into her robe, splashes her face with water, and goes to the kitchen.

"I'm sorry," Annie says, handing her a mug of black coffee. "When I invited the group here for brunch, I thought it would be your only chance to meet them. I didn't know we'd be seeing them last night too."

Betty grins as she settles in at the table. "Hmmm," she says. "I guess that's why they call it a surprise party."

The bacon, frying in the skillet, sounds like splattering rain. Annie turns it over and smiles. "I know. I still can't believe they'd do that for me. But first the party and now this . . . It can't be much fun for you, spending your whole weekend with people you barely know."

"For goodness' sakes, Annie, I'm having a wonderful time. I like your friends."

"They're great, aren't they?" Annie says, pouring orange juice into a pitcher. "But I'd counted on us having more time together. Do you really have to leave today?"

Betty takes a sip of her coffee. "I don't want to, but I have to."

"Why do you have to?" Annie says, drilling her with her eyes. "You already said you don't have to be back to work 'til Tuesday."

"I know, but—"

"But what? What's so important it can't wait one more day?"

Betty sighs as she sets the table with place mats, napkins, and silverware. What did she have to do at home that was so important? The minute she walked through the door it would be the same old same old. Mama Dean would glare at her, then start fussing about her gallivanting, Gladys Spivey's latest insult, Maggie ruining her life, then they'd go on to Jill going downhill in a handbasket. Later, Mama Dean would doze in front of the TV, while Betty spent another boring Sunday straightening the house, clipping two-for-one coupons from the newspaper, then catching up on the ironing. But now that she's seen Annie's life she realizes what she's been missing. And when Charlie Love, and the possibility of him, floats into her mind, the thought of going home makes her want to lay her head on the table and cry.

"Oh, Annie," she says. "What about Mama Dean?"

"No problem. Just call her."

"You don't understand. I'd feel guilty as homemade sin."

"Guilty!" Annie says. "Why should you feel guilty? You're always there for her. You do everything for her."

"Well, Lord, Annie. She *is* my mother, you know."

"I know she is, bless your heart."

"Well, for goodness' sake, Annie."

"I'm sorry. But you've got to admit she's turned being a difficult woman into an art form and it's just getting worse."

Betty laughs, then feels depressed again. "I know. But she isn't getting any younger."

"None of us is getting any younger! Besides, you said yourself that Jill's staying with her. Mama Dean isn't exactly an invalid, you know. She's probably setting up a poker game right now."

"Bingo."

"What?"

"Friday night's poker. Sunday is bingo."

"You've got to be kidding! Here you are feeling guilty while Mama Dean's having the time of her life. Come on, Betty, we're just talking one more day. The last time I saw you was at Ed's funeral. That was three years ago. This time I wanted us to have a real visit. After everyone leaves we can walk on the beach, come back here for a nice dinner, drink a little wine, have us some girl talk."

Betty ducks her head. It all sounded so simple. But if Annie thought Jill staying with Mama Dean was any comfort, she didn't know Mama Dean. Even before she'd left home the air was prickly with tension. Mama Dean followed Jill through the house, timing her phone calls, turning off lights, or standing outside the bathroom while Jill showered, and announcing, loudly, "Some people seem to think water grows on trees."

So what if Mama Dean spent a couple of hours at bingo? That still gave her fourteen hours a day to fuss and argue with Jill. Annie was right. Mama Dean was getting more and more difficult. For years she'd been able to joke about it. "You think your mother's impossible," she'd say to her friends at work. "Wait'll you hear what Mama Dean did." Then she'd tell her story and watch everyone's jaws drop.

But lately it didn't seem the least bit funny. Betty had spent too much of her life trying to smooth things over, while Mama Dean seemed more and more determined to stir things up. What if she wasn't there, and things went too far? Jill was already upset. What if Mama Dean started in on Maggie and Steven? What if she repeated gossip about their breakup? What if she called Jill a hippie once too often, and the girl stomped off in a huff?

Betty sighs. It is hard to believe that just ten minutes ago, she thought her life had taken a turn. Annie. The beach. Charlie Love. Last night she'd felt something special between them. But if she leaves right after brunch she'll probably never see him again. Will she spend the rest of her life wondering how it could have been if she'd stayed another day? And Annie. She hasn't seen Annie for years and it had taken Ed's death to get her there, then. Now she's rushing off. Hurting Annie's feelings. "Oh," she wails. "I don't know what to do."

Annie sighs, then goes back to wiping off counters, setting out juice glasses. Finally she turns. "Listen, Betty. I don't mean to over-step my bounds, but we've been friends a long time, and I've just gotta say it. There are some things in this world worth fighting for. And a few days away now and then is one of them. If you really want to stay, then stay. I know payback is hell, and Mama Dean'll proba-bly sulk around the house for a while, but she'll get over it."

"You think so?"

"I guaran-damn-tee it. I mean, what's she gonna do? Kick you out?"

"I should be so lucky," Betty mutters, and they both laugh.

"That's the spirit," Annie says. "Now, take a deep breath and call her."

"All right, all right, I'll call. But, darn it, Annie, you sure like to get me in hot water."

Annie grins in triumph. "Oh, well," she says. "At least it's not stagnant water."

The brunch is subdued. Everyone is tired and out of conversation after last night's party. At noon, when they start saying their good-byes, Betty takes a deep breath, then forgets to exhale as Charlie stands up with the others. He'd been by her side all morning, smiled at everything she said, even patted her arm and told funny, affec-tionate stories about his own mother when Annie teased her about Mama Dean. But now he is leaving, without a word about seeing her again.

She'd been a fool to think there was something special between them! He was just being nice, the perfect English gentleman. She was a backward, small-town hick to have read anything more into it.

She says good-bye at the door, then stays on the porch while Annie goes outside to see everyone off. But when the cars start backing out of the driveway, sudden tears sting her eyes and she goes back inside to pull herself together.

"Idiot!" she mutters, as she slams a skillet into the sink and attacks it with an S.O.S pad. "What did you expect?"

Then, suddenly, she hears laughter, a man's voice saying, "You don't think we'd leave you and Betty to clean up alone, do you, love?"

"There's nothing I like better than a man in the kitchen," Annie says. "But as soon as we finish, y'all have to scoot. I've only got one day to spend with Betty."

And before she can take it all in, Charlie, Annie, and Sam Maddox are back in the kitchen.

The radio is playing and Annie hums and moves her hips to the music while she fills the sink with hot, sudsy water. Then Sam slips up behind her, takes her in his arms and they do an odd, combination two-step, tango across the room.

Everyone is laughing as Annie dances back to the sink. "Y'all hafta excuse Sam. He's crazy," she says, plunging her hands into the dishwater. Then, all at once there's a strange popping sound and Annie's voice sounds hollow and tinny. "Oh, gosh! I'm bleeding!"

They gather around her. There's a broken glass in the sink—a surprising amount of blood. "I need a clean towel," Betty says. She checks Annie's hand, runs it under cold water, then examines it closely. There are scratches crisscrossing the back of her hand, but a cut at the base of her thumb is deep and jagged.

"My hand was inside the glass when it broke," Annie says. Her face is pale. Betty remembers that Annie was a fainter back in nursing school. She wraps the hand in the towel then guides Annie to a chair. "You need to go to the emergency room, hon."

Annie looks stricken. "But it's your last day and now it's ruined. Can't you butterfly it?"

Betty shakes her head as Sam, who'd disappeared for a moment, returns with his car keys and Annie's purse. "Come on, Annie. You know it needs stitches."

As they walk her to Sam's car, Annie wails, "But we were gonna go to the beach, do all kinds of stuff. Oh, Betty, promise you won't leave while I'm gone."

"But I thought I was going with you," Betty stammers.

"No," Annie says stubbornly. "You are not spending your day off from the hospital in a hospital waiting room! Charlie?"

"Don't worry, love. I won't let her out of my sight. We'll have everything cleared up by the time you get back. You and Betty can still have your day."

Then suddenly they are gone and Betty stands blinking in the driveway. She had wanted to spend more time with Charlie. But now, instead of being thrilled, she feels guilty and embarrassed. Guilty because Annie got hurt. Embarrassed because she doesn't know if Charlie wants to stay or if he's staying because he promised Annie.

Her face feels flushed as she follows him inside. It doesn't help that the breakfast nook is so small they have to sidestep each other as they clear the table. At times he's so close, she can smell the faint, sweet scent of his soap, feel the heat of his body as he brushes against her reaching for a platter or bowl. She makes feeble stabs at conversation, Annie's injury, last night's party, the blueberry muffins at brunch. But Charlie's so quiet and distracted that soon they are saying little more than, "excuse me," "thank you" and "here, let me get that for you."

Betty leaves the breakfast nook for the safe haven of the kitchen. Maybe working in the next room—keeping him out of her sight—will save her. She loads the silverware into the dishwasher while she tries to find a tactful way to say, "You don't have to stay." But before she can think of a way to say it, Charlie comes into the room, sets a stack of dishes on the counter, and turns to her. "I'm sorry. I know I'm being awkward. But did you ever hear the expression, 'Be careful what you wish?'"

Betty nods.

He takes off his glasses and rubs the bridge of his nose. "I'll probably make a real hash of this. But I spent all weekend hoping . . . wishing for something to happen so I could spend more time with you. Then the brunch was over and I hadn't so much as asked if I could call you. I came back to help clean up. To stall for time, really. But, then Annie got hurt and now all I can think is be careful what you wish. Do ya know what I mean, love?"

And Betty, who has always been shy around men, who sometimes wondered if she even liked them very much, finds herself saying, "Charlie Love, that's got to be the nicest thing I've ever heard."

19

Jill

....

On Sunday morning, Jill and Freedom wait around the corner from Jill's house until her father and sister drive past them on the way to church. As soon as the family car turns the corner, Jill backs Mama Dean's baby-blue Pinto into the driveway.

"Okay," she says. "Let's synchronize our watches. We've got an hour, maybe an hour and fifteen minutes, to get the carvings for the flea market."

Freedom's face is pale. "Oh, my God! This is wild," she says. "First we steal your great-grandmother's car and now we're breaking and entering."

That's when Jill starts to get nervous. "Nobody's forcing you to do this," she snaps.

"No," Freedom says. "I mean it's like cool-wild. This is good. Great even. It feels like that movie *Butch Cassidy and the Sundance Kid*."

"Yeah. Butch and Sundance in a seventy-six Pinto."

Freedom laughs. "Yeah, but it's not just your everyday Pinto.

Leave it to your great-grandma to have a bicentennial Pinto with red, white, and blue racing stripes."

They're still laughing when they get out of the car and walk toward the garage workshop. It isn't until Jill digs the key out of her jeans pocket that she sees something is wrong. The padlock is in place, wedged tightly through the latch like always, but it's hanging at an odd, twisted angle. She reaches out and grabs it. "Oh, no! Somebody's cut the lock!"

Her heart is pounding as she jiggles the lock, then yanks on it, trying to force it up through the hasp. But her hands are shaky and sweaty, and the lock is old and rusty. She wipes her hands on her jeans legs, takes a deep, ragged breath, and tries again. This time she pulls the padlock up as far as it will go, smacks it with the heel of her hand, and pops it free.

For a moment she just stands there, feeling her body sway, as a deep sense of foreboding washes over her.

"Jill?" Freedom says.

"This is scaring the shit out of me," she says, closing her eyes. "You go first. I can't stand it."

She holds her breath, feels herself flinch as she hears the door swing open, then the sounds of gritting footsteps. Now, Freedom is shouting, "Geeza, Louisa! Where are we gonna put all this stuff? The totem pole alone is six foot tall."

Jill hesitates, then goes inside. Her eyes dart everywhere, taking in the whole room. For a moment it looks just like it did when she left it. Then, she notices that a lower shelf is empty; wood scraps she'd saved for small projects have been swept into a pile in the corner, and the basket of adobe houses, her moneymakers, has been knocked on its side, scattering dozens of the tiny carvings onto the floor.

She looks around wildly, then hurries from one end of the narrow room to the other. Suddenly she stops. "Oh, God," she wails. "The Medicine Woman!"

Freedom comes up behind her. "Come on, Jill. We'll find her. It's gonna be all right."

Jill turns on her, "It is not all right. She was right here on the workbench and now she's gone!"

It's probably only seconds, but it seems like several long minutes before they find a box jammed under a lower shelf, filled with the missing carvings. A few moments later, Jill spots the medicine woman, wedged on a shelf behind an Indian chief. Tears sting her eyes as she cradles the carving in her arms and runs her fingers over every surface.

"I hate him! I mean it. We've got to get everything out of here before he does something awful."

Freedom's kohl-lined eyes look like burn holes in a blanket in her pale face. "I don't get it. Why would he do something like this?"

Jill's chest feels tight. Her throat hurts. "Because it's his house and he thinks this is bullshit. He thinks everything important to me is bullshit. But this is my stuff. Mine. He's got no right to come in here and trash it. Come on, Freedom. We've got to hurry!"

She's still bawling as she runs back to the car and pulls boxes and bungees from the hatchback. She wipes her eyes with the backs of her hands and concentrates on clearing the shelves. They work quickly, methodically, at first: a separate box for the medicine woman, which will ride on Freedom's lap; another box for the bird carvings, then the small animal carvings. When they run out of boxes they start scooping up armloads and dumping them into trash bags and grocery sacks—anything they can find—piling them in the hatchback from floorboard to roof; wedging chisels, hammers, and adzes tightly between the seats.

When the workshop is empty, they carry the totem pole outside and set it in the driveway.

Jill stares at the house. For a moment all she wants to do is go back in time, to the days when her mother hummed in the kitchen while she browned Sunday's roast, to a time when she still thought it was possible to make her father proud. But that was never going to happen. No matter how hard she tried, her father ended every disagreement by slamming into his den, shouting, "As long as you're under my roof, you'll do what I say." Now her mother is gone. Jill is staying with Grandy and Mama Dean. Even Amy, the perfect twin, has sworn that after she goes off to college she'll never come back. Soon her father will be the only one under this roof. Maybe then he'll have everything the way he wants it. Maybe then he'll be happy.

"It's getting late, Jill," Freedom says. "Are you ready?"

"Yeah," she says, quietly. "I've been ready for years."

Then she and Freedom hoist the six-foot-tall totem pole onto the roof of the car.

20

Mama Dean

. . . .

The telephone is ringing as Mama Dean comes in the back door from church.

"Who in the world?" she mutters. She drops her purse and church bulletin on the kitchen table, then in her hurry to answer, she clangs the receiver against her glasses, knocking them side-goggly.

"Hmmph," she says, straightening them.

"Mrs. Pruitt, this is Steven Presson. I want to know what's going on with my daughter."

The voice is familiar, but she's out of breath and confused. She pauses, rubs the bridge of her nose, then smiles. "They Lord, Steven, is that you?"

"You know very well it's me," he says coldly. "I want to know what you and your family are trying to do, encouraging my daughter to make a fool out of me."

"Well, Steven, I never . . ." she stammers.

"Yeah, right," he says, flicking off her words like a dog flicking off a flea. "Don't try to deny it. A neighbor saw your car and called me."

"Steven Presson," she says, as shocked as if he'd slapped her. "I'll thank you not to talk to me like that. I did not know it was you and I don't know what you're talking about. Now, if you'll call back and try to act like you're somebody, I might consider answering the phone."

She slams down the receiver and sinks onto a chair at the kitchen table, fanning herself with the church bulletin. Why, the very idea of him calling her like that, expecting her to know who he was! How could she have known? He was family. He'd called her Mama Dean ever since he'd married Maggie. Now, here he was calling her Mrs. Pruitt, like a stranger, or a bill collector, or someone from the I. R. of S. She'd never heard him so hateful and snotty. He'd all but called her a liar. Accusing her of Lord knows what and her barely in the door from church!

She stares out the kitchen window, gnaws her bottom lip, and fans herself a little harder.

"Well, Steven Presson," she says out loud. "I ain't putting up with any of your S.B. I've defended you all over hell and half of Georgia, but now you can kiss my foot!"

She stops fanning, takes a deep breath, and blows it out again. Now he'd done it—caused her to cuss on a Sunday. But a call like that was enough to make a preacher cuss, much less an old woman with her nerves all torn to pieces and her low sugar blood making her swimmy-headed.

She takes the lid off the cut-glass candy dish in the middle of the table, and pops a fistful of M&M's into her mouth. Then another. Dr. Pinckney would have a fit if he knew she was eating candy. But Dr. Pinckney didn't need to know everything. Why, with all that was going on in the family, it was a pure wonder she hadn't taken up dope.

The phone rings again, but she just chews a ragged cuticle, stares out the window and fans. She counts the rings, nine, ten, eleven, then she picks up the receiver and slams it back into its cradle.

"Hmmph, Mr. Fancy Britches," she mutters. "How do you like that?"

The phone rings again. This time she glares at it, picks up the receiver, and stuffs it in the drawer with the dish towels. Steven's words sound like angry, pent-up bees as she slams the drawer on them.

Her head is throbbing. She rubs her temples and the back of her neck. "Law, me. I need to take a Tylenol—get me a bite to eat."

She crosses the room to the refrigerator, opens the door, and looks inside. She is spreading mayonnaise on a bologna sandwich when she sees a parade float drift up the street, come to a lumbering halt in front of the house, then make a wide left turn into the driveway.

She blinks, refocuses her eyes, and looks again.

Havemercy! It isn't a parade float after all. It's her car, riding low, with boxes stacked in every window, top-heavy and swaying from the weight of a painted log on the roof.

The car lists haltingly past the window, and for the first time she sees that Jill is driving and that Freda girl, riding shotgun in the passenger seat, is egging her on.

She stands there for a moment, staring with her mouth dropped opened. Then she stomps through to the front room, wraps the couch afghan around her shoulders, and marches to the back porch.

"Jill Kayroley Presson," she shouts. "This time I'm fixing to cut me a switch!"

21

Jill

. . . .

"Holy shit," Freedom says, as Mama Dean shakes her fist, then starts down the driveway after them. "We're busted."

Jill clenches her jaw, tightens her grip on the steering wheel, then keeps going, past the picnic table, the bird bath, a small cluster of cedars.

Freedom's voice is shrill. "What're you trying to do, outrun her? Stop, Jill! Stop the car!"

Jill eases on the brakes, then comes to a complete stop near the shed. "Oh, God, I'm toast."

"Get out of the car. Try to act normal."

Jill's ears are ringing. She sees spots before her eyes. "Normal! You've gotta be kidding! You've never seen Mama Dean pissed off."

"Well, she'll be twice as pissed if she has to walk clear back here. Come on. We'll think of something."

Jill groans. "I *think* I'm gonna throw up." As she opens the door to get out, boxes and carvings shift, then tumble over the backseat onto the driver's seat, the floor, then onto the ground. She watches her feet, trying not to stumble or step on anything, then she raises up too quickly and bangs her head on the totem pole lashed to the roof.

For a moment, all in the world she wants to do is fall on the ground and pretend she's unconscious, but Freedom grabs her arm and hisses, "Come on."

Jill blinks as they start up the rise toward the driveway. She sees steam radiating from Mama Dean. She blinks again, then realizes that it isn't just Mama Dean; everything around her is blurry.

Jill's mind flashes to the time when she was nine or ten and her father came to her bedroom. He said he was going to spank her, then he made her get the hairbrush from the dresser and carry it to him. He had spanked her before; a few quick, sudden pops that were over in an instant, with no time to think about it. But it was the knowing what was about to happen that made her legs turn to mush. Later, she could never remember her crime or the actual spanking, just the slow, drawn-out torture as each step brought her closer to doom.

Now Mama Dean is twenty feet away and glaring.

"Oh, God. What'll I do?"

"It'll be all right. I'll do the talking," Freedom says. "I think she likes me."

And before Jill can shout, "Are you crazy? Have you lost your freaking mind?" Freedom calls out, "Hey, Mrs. Pruitt, how're you doing?" Just like Eddie Haskell on *Leave It to Beaver*.

Mama Dean doesn't answer. She just hitches the afghan higher on her shoulders and keeps walking. All at once, she's just inches away. Her eyes are blazing and her chin is jutted out. "Don't you all 'hey' me. I want to know what in the Sam Hill you think you're doing with my car."

Jill freezes.

Freedom glances at the car, then makes a nervous sound that's meant to pass for laughter. "Well ma'am, we used it to pick up some school supplies."

Jill stares at Freedom. She can't believe what she's said. And from the way her jaw drops, neither can Mama Dean. For a moment Mama Dean looks confused, then she turns toward Freedom.

"Get home, sister, before I call your daddy. And you," she says, grabbing Jill's arm. "Get in the house."

Jill's face feels hot as Mama Dean hauls her up the driveway.

For a while Freedom follows, calling out, "Honest, Mrs. Pruitt, they *are* school supplies. Art-school supplies. Jill's gotta have 'em for her class with Chief Too-Tall."

But Mama Dean ignores her. She just stomps up the porch steps, and doesn't let go of Jill until they are inside the house and Freedom has drifted toward home.

"Oh, God," Jill wails, as this whole long, impossible day catches up with her. All she wants to do is run to her room before she really starts crying. But as she heads toward the hall, Mama Dean shouts, "Hey, you, get back here."

Jill freezes. All her life she's heard stories about her grandmother's temper, but this is the first time she's seen it.

"I said get back here. And don't you ever 'Oh, God' me."

"I didn't 'Oh, God' you, I just . . ."

"There you go, doing it again, and me standing right here telling you not to cuss."

"But, Mama Dean . . . I . . ."

"Hush," Mama Dean says, as she sinks heavily into the rocking chair. "Don't say another word. Now, you set yourself down, Miss

Twitchy Britches, and don't even think about moving 'til I tell you."

Jill finds a seat on the couch, as far from her grandmother as possible.

Except for the sounds of the rocking chair, the room is silent. Jill stares at the floor, but every now and then she steals a glance at Mama Dean, who is moving her lips and rocking for all she is worth. Jill wonders if she's praying or gathering up steam to launch into a pure fit. Then, suddenly, Mama Dean stops rocking and the room goes so still that Jill can hear the whir of the ceiling fan and the refrigerator hum. When the clock cuckoos, she jumps as if she's been shot.

Finally Mama Dean speaks, and her voice is low and mournful. "It's the Bible fulfilling itself. There'll be weeping and wailing and gnashing of teeth on Judgment Day." Then she looks at Jill as if she's expecting her to say something.

Jill's mind goes blank. If her grandmother is starting the conversation with weeping and wailing they could be here all day. But she has to take whatever's being dished out. She needs a place to stay and she needs Mama Dean's help.

"I just never thought I'd live to see the day my own granddaughter would steal from me and her daddy."

Jill has been trying to keep Mama Dean's voice in the background like a radio turned low, but now she's jerked back to reality. "What do you mean stealing from Daddy?"

Mama Dean stops rocking. "He called a while ago. He was all tore up. Got me all tore up. I never heard him take on so."

Tears sting Jill's eyes as she leaps from the couch and starts pacing the room. "I didn't steal from him. It was my stuff. Mine! Oh, Mama Dean, it's not fair. He was trashing everything. I had to get it out of there."

Mama Dean narrows her eyes. "So you decided to steal the man's firewood to get back at him?"

Jill stops pacing and stares at her. "Firewood?"

"The firewood stacked on the roof of the car . . . my car that you stole."

For a moment it's as if her grandmother is speaking Swahili or Russian, some language so foreign it has a different alphabet. Then Jill pictures the car's roof and everything clicks into place.

"You mean the totem pole? Mama Dean, that's not firewood, it's a wood carving. *My* carving. I've carved dozens of things. Daddy was fixing to throw them all out."

Mama Dean leans back and closes her eyes. "Law, me," she says. "I think I'm taking the headache."

Jill goes out to the kitchen and returns with Tylenol and a glass of water. Mama Dean glares at her, but takes the pills.

"Wood carvings?" she says, frowning. "You mean whittling?"

"Something like that, only bigger. More like sculptures or statues . . . you know, art." Jill is smiling, warming to her subject when Mama Dean holds her hand up like a traffic cop.

"Hmmph," she says. "I don't want to hear none of that art folderol. Art never paid the rent nor put food on the table. It's as useless as tits on a bull. But if it means that much to you, you might as well store it in my shed so your daddy won't bother it."

Tears sting Jill's eyes. "Thanks, Mama Dean. You don't know what that means to me."

Mama Dean stops rocking and looks at her. Then her chin quivers and her eyes well. "Lordamercy, child, what did you expect. *You're* my great-granddaughter. You're the one's blood and bone to me."

22

Wednesday evening, when Betty gets home from work, the house is silent. She goes from room to room looking for Jill and Mama Dean. When she sees that she's really alone, she does a small dance of joy, heads back to the kitchen, and dials the phone.

An alto voice says, "Hey, Chicapay."

Betty laughs. "What in the world's a chickapay?"

Annie laughs too. "I don't know. I just saw that movie *Nell.* Jodie Foster kept saying 'Chickapay' and it cracked me up. So, how're you? Is Jill still staying with you all? Is Mama Dean letting you out of the house yet?"

"Mama Dean gave me her 'gallivanting Betty' speech the minute I walked through the door. But other than that it's been quiet. I can't decide if they declared some kind of truce while I was gone or if they're just laying low. Whatever it is, I like it. Course I probably just jinxed it by talking about it. But how are you? How's your hand?"

"It's healing. Slow as molasses, but it's healing. It aggravates me to death that it had to happen on your last day here."

"Stop worrying about that. I'm just glad it's getting better."

"Me too," Annie says. "And I'm glad it gave you and a certain Englishman a chance to spend time together."

Betty had called to check on Annie's hand and to thank her for the weekend. Sooner or later she'd planned to find a way to work Charlie into the conversation. Now she feels like a fool. Leave it to Annie to throw her off balance by reading her mind and blurting it out.

"You mean Charlie?" Betty stammers, as if he's the furthest thing from her mind, as if she spent time with so many men, that a three-day-old meeting with a certain Englishman is only a vague memory.

"Of course I mean Charlie! Come on, Betty. Give. I was the one who brought you together. Now, I'm dying to know what's going on."

Betty's face feels flushed. "Nothing's going on," she says, keeping her voice casual. "We met. It was fun. The end."

"Uh-huh."

"If I'm lying, I'm dying."

"You mean he hasn't called you?"

"I haven't heard nary a word."

"He will. I never saw the beat of it. The two of you were lit up like Christmas all weekend."

Betty smiles. "You think so?"

"I know so. Even Sam's talking about it."

"Sam! You and Sam were talking about us?"

"Well, sure. Wait 'til I tell him Charlie hasn't called you yet."

"Don't you dare! Don't you dare say a thing to Sam or anyone else. I mean it! I'd feel like a fool—like a child passing notes in grade school. My friend likes you. Do you like her? Check yes or no." Betty shouts, startling herself.

"Well, I swan. Are you all right?"

"Oh, Lord. I didn't mean to jump all over you. But, please, whatever you do, promise you won't say anything. I don't want any fix-ups. If Charlie wants to call, he'll call."

"Okay!"

"Promise."

"All right, I promise. I didn't mean to upset you. You really do like him, don't you?"

Betty pauses, not sure where to begin, but before she can answer, there's a beep on the line. "Hold on, Annie. It's my call waiting. Probably Mama Dean needing to be picked up." She clicks the line over.

"Still me," Annie says.

"Sorry," she says, clicking over again.

"Still me," Annie says.

She clicks over again. This time the air is so dead for a moment she thinks she's lost both the caller and Annie. "Damn," she mutters into the receiver.

Then a man says, "Betty? Have I picked a bad time to call you, love?"

Her heart gives a lurch. Charlie's finally called and she'd cursed into the phone. She takes a deep breath and pulls herself together. "Hey, Charlie. Can you hold on a second?"

Betty clicks the line over. "Annie," she whispers. "It's Charlie."

"Is he there?"

"He's on the other line."

"Why are you whispering?"

"I don't know!"

"Call me back. I mean it. Call me back."

Betty clicks the line over again. "Well, Charlie, this must be beach day. I was just talking to Annie."

"I did pick a bad time, then, didn't I? Let me call you back."

"It's all right. We were about to hang up when your call came through. So, how are you?"

"I'm fine, love. But, the thing is, I'm not calling from the beach. I'm at my son's place."

"That's nice."

"It is, isn't it. Actually, Betty, my son lives in Charlotte, about a half hour from you."

When Betty arrives at the Curl & Swirl, Maggie meets her at the door, pulls her inside, and whispers, "Let's go to the back, so we can talk."

Betty follows her to the back of the shop, and sits on the edge of a shampoo chair.

"You really want me to shampoo you?" Maggie says.

"Well, sure. You said you'd work me in at four-thirty."

"You don't have to make an appointment to see me, you know."

Betty is confused. "But I want my hair done."

"Really? I thought something was wrong. You hardly ever get your hair done and I just did it last week. I figured what with Mama Dean and all . . . well, I thought something had happened and the only way you could think to see me was to come to the shop."

"I didn't mean to worry you. I just have a . . . uh . . . special dinner tonight. But everything's fine. Jill's not saying much, but I think she's all right."

Maggie takes another deep breath and gets busy. She covers Betty with a cape, tilts the chair over the shampoo bowl. "Your color looks good." Then, "Tell me if the water's too hot."

Betty closes her eyes and tries to relax.

"I've had so much on my mind," Maggie says, as she massages apple pectin shampoo into Betty's scalp. "I forgot to ask about your trip to Annie's."

Betty squeezes her eyes tight, and smiles. "It was great. I didn't know how much I needed a break."

Maggie rinses her hair, wraps it in a towel, then raises the chair. "And Annie? How's she doing?"

"Annie's great. She's met someone."

"You mean a man?"

"Yes, I mean a man. Is there something wrong with that?"

"Gosh, no! I'm just surprised. Annie's just always been so, well, no offense, Mother, but she's always been so . . . uh . . . grandmotherly. Plus she was married to Ed for a thousand years. It's just hard to think of her with someone else."

"Annie's only fifty-seven."

"I know she is, bless her heart. I guess she misses the companionship."

Betty laughs. "For heaven's sake, Maggie. Annie's not ready for side-by-side rocking chairs yet. She's dyed her hair red, wears size eight outfits she calls rompers, and the last time I saw her, she and her 'companion' were tangoing across the kitchen."

"Good grief, Mother! Do you think they're serious?"

Betty sits up in her chair, and blots her hair with the towel. "Oh, Maggie, you should have seen them. They have such a good time together, and they're so . . . I don't know . . . I guess tender is the word. They're so tender with each other."

Suddenly Charlie floats into Betty's mind and she feels her face flush. She glances at Maggie just in time to see Maggie glance at her then look away.

"Come on up front so I can blow-dry your hair."

Maggie is quiet as she rubs in the mousse, then combs it through. Finally she says. "Do you ever think about it, Mother?"

"Think about what?"

"You know, having someone special?"

"What makes you ask that?"

"I don't know. I was just thinking about that night I had a fight with the girls and came over to cry on your shoulder."

"Uh-huh."

"It was the first time I'd seen us as two grown-up women, not just mother and daughter, you know? You were so open that night. So different. You were even dressed different. Ever since I can remember you've dressed like Betty-the-nurse."

"What's that supposed to mean?"

"Knit pants and knit shirts. White in the summer. Off-white in the winter. You know, that well-scrubbed look."

"Well, for goodness' sakes."

Maggie smiles. "But that night you were wearing a soft, floaty dress and bare feet and the house smelled of lavender. Then, just before I left, you got a phone call from a man. A man with an English accent. And all I could think was, oh my, what if my own little mama has a whole secret life I never knew about?"

Betty's face feels hot. "I guess I should tell you . . . the dinner I'm going to tonight . . . I've got a date."

"What?"

"I've got a date."

In the mirror, Betty can see Maggie's jaw drop and her eyes go wide.

Betty looks away.

"Well, for goodness' sakes, Mother! Is it someone I know?"

"I met him at Annie's."

Neither of them say anything for a while. Finally Maggie says, "Is it the man on the phone? The one with the English accent?"

Betty nods. "We hadn't even met then. We'd talked on the phone a few times about some old photos for Annie's party and now we've got a date."

Maggie's voice sounds hollow and faraway. "Well, for goodness' sakes, Mother, for goodness' sakes!"

Dear Annie,

This will have to be quick. I'm on my lunch break at work.

You said you wanted details, so here goes. Charlie has been here every night this week. We go out to supper. Sometimes we'll take a walk or just drive around and talk. Honestly, Annie, it's hard to believe I've only known him a few weeks the way we can talk about everything.

You should have seen the look on Mama Dean's face the first time he came to pick me up. I'd told her I was going out with a friend, but had put off telling her it was a man friend until the last minute. (You know how Mama Dean feels about men!) But then Charlie was early and I was still in my room getting ready when he got here.

Jill told me later that when he knocked on the door Mama Dean came up out of her chair like it had given her an electric shock. Then he started to talk and her jaw dropped and her face went red. (I still don't know what he said. Jill couldn't understand the first word!) Anyway, that night, Mama Dean waited up for me and the minute I came in she said, "I guess you know he's some kind of foreigner."

Charlie can tell she isn't exactly warming up to him, so he's making a big fuss over her. All but courting her. Like the other night, I mentioned that she likes chow-chow, and the next day, on his way to pick me up, he stopped at the Cracker Barrel and bought her some. It's so sweet the way he goes out of his way to win her over. I hate to tell him it probably won't happen, because (1) he's a man, and (2) he isn't even southern.

I didn't know that his son took over his landscaping business when he retired and that the business is in Charlotte. Charlie goes there for a week every month to help out with the payroll and inventory. As the kids say, "It works for me!" He's heading back home tomorrow, but we already have plans for three weeks from today.

Jill's been a big help, keeping Mama Dean company and driving her places. I don't know what I'd do without her, what with working days and seeing Charlie every night. I'm really going to miss her when she goes home, then off to school. Though now that I think about it she hasn't mentioned home or school in ages. And her daddy hasn't so much as called to check on her, which I think is awful. I guess I need to find out what's going on.

Well, Annie, I gotta go. Take care of your hand and say "hey" to Sam for me.

Love,
Betty

P.S. Maggie says I dress like Betty-the-nurse. Do you think beads would help?

P.S. #2 I forgot to tell you. The other night, before Jill went to bed, she said, "Good night, Grandy, love," and she said it in an English accent. Wouldn't you know the one person who's on my side is leaving soon.

P.S. #3 We have not been necking at Belews Pond! I can't believe you'd ask such a thing.

23

Jill

....

It's been a slow day at the flea market. Jill is alone in her booth after sending Freedom to spy on Make Mine Country in building G.

She's bent over the display table, packing up for the day, when she sees her mother coming up the aisle toward her.

"I don't believe it," she mutters.

For a moment she considers hiding under the table. But it's too late for that. Her mother is waving and calling out, "Hey, Jill!"

Jill's face feels hot. That was the trouble with flea markets. They had to let anyone in. First it was Daddy and Mrs. Bloodworth. But at least she'd seen them coming while there was still time to hide. Leave it to Mama to sneak up and surprise her. She turns her back, concentrates on packing the carvings, and tries to pull herself together. But her mother is standing at the table, oblivious to her signals, as if she belongs here, as if she were a paying customer and welcomed here.

Jill dives under the display cloth, and takes a long time rearranging bags and boxes. Maybe if she ignores her, her mother will go away.

But when she crawls out from under the table, her mother is still waiting. Jill keeps her head down, as she focuses on wrapping the smaller carvings in newspaper. Finally she takes a deep breath and says, "What do you want, Mama?"

But before her mother can answer, Freedom appears. She looks pale and confused, as she stares at Maggie then Jill, then Jill and Maggie.

"I need to pee," Jill says, then she picks up her purse and stomps off toward the rest room.

She hides out in the farthest stall and stares at the graffiti on the wall. BRANDY'S A BITCH. TREY AND LINDSEY, TOGETHER 4EVER. She is pulling a felt-tip pen from her purse when she hears the door swing open and her mother call, "Jill, are you in here?"

Jill ignores her. Under the legend JESUS SAVES she writes AT FIRST UNION BANK.

"Jill, I know you're in here. We need to talk."

"No shit!" Jill mutters, under her breath. Then, she slams out of the stall, stalks past her mother, and bangs the rest-room door behind her.

As she darts up the aisle toward her booth, she catches Freedom's eye, then points toward an exit to signal she's leaving. She makes it across the parking lot before the tears that are stinging her eyes start to spill over. "Dammit, Mama. Dammit!"

Grandy is working a split shift and Mama Dean is at the V.F.W. playing bingo. Jill has the house to herself. She's washing supper dishes while she waits to hear from Freedom. When it hits her that Freedom should have called by now, she crosses the kitchen and dials the phone.

"It's me," she says. "Are we going out or what?"

Freedom's voice is faint. "I'm not speaking to you."

"What'd I do?"

"Duh."

"Come on, Freedom. Tell me!"

"I can't believe you don't know. It was bad enough you took off like that. But I thought for sure you'd come back."

"God, Freedom, you saw what happened. My mom showing up and all. Besides it was almost closing time and I'd already covered most of the stuff."

"Big deal! It's *your* stuff. You left me to pack everything and haul it to the van. It was awful. Then, your mom came out of the rest room and she looked so sad. Honest to God, Jill, I felt sorry for her."

Jill feels her insides shift. "Don't even go there. I don't want to talk about her."

"But she's your mom. You can't stay mad forever."

"Oh, yeah? Just watch me."

For a while neither of them says anything. Finally Jill says, "I'm sorry about leaving you in a mess."

"You should be."

"Don't be mad. I said I'm sorry. Tell me what happened?"

"What do you wanna hear first? The bad news or the worst news."

"You're freaking me out."

"Freaking out's a good place to start."

"Come on, Freedom, just say it."

"All right. All right. First off, we're broke."

"How broke?"

"We barely made enough to pay for the booth. Then, just before closing, the owner, you know, the skinny one with the pointy nose, the one who wears the whistle around her neck . . ."

"Ferret-face?"

"That's it! Well, just before closing, she came around to the tables to tell us she's raising the rent."

"You've got to be kidding."

"I wish. But that's not all. Remember when you sent me to spy on Make Mine Country, but we didn't get to talk because your mom showed up? Well, they're doing so great next week they're moving to that huge hut in building A."

After she hangs up, Jill goes out the back door, crosses the yard, ducks behind the tool shed, and lights a cigarette. It wasn't fair. She'd worked so hard and could barely afford a tiny booth in building H while Make Mine Country, which sold nothing but crap, was making *beaucoup* money. Still, if she ever wanted her own place and classes with the chief, she had to find a way to compete. Maybe it was time to swallow her pride and give the people what they wanted, even if it was geese and gnomes. But what if she came up with her own line of country carvings? Picasso-style geese. Art-deco gnomes. But that was the problem. They'd still be originals and people didn't seem to want originals. They wanted cutouts of boys pissing into the bushes. Women bending over, showing polka-dotted bloomers. Plastic pink flamingos. Jill rubs her temples. Just thinking about making junk like that makes her want to shout, Cop out, sell out, loser.

And speaking of losers, what was Mama doing showing up like that? Did she think Jill would be too embarrassed to make a scene in public? That they'd fling themselves into each other's arms, while the vendors and customers applauded, like one of those Sally Jesse Raphael reunion shows or something?

She is puffing on her cigarette and staring off into space when she hears a car pull into the driveway. She peeks out from behind the tool shed and sees her father's gray LTD, but it's Amy, dressed like a page out of some preppy handbook, who gets out of the car.

Jill looks down at her own dusty bare feet, her grubby bib overalls and faded tie-dyed T-shirt. She considers putting out the cigarette and brushing herself off, but suddenly she's too tired to care. She steps out into the yard and holds up the cigarette, "Hey, Amy, you've got to love it. You busted me fair and square."

Amy wrinkles her nose as she walks toward her. "Like I didn't know. Honestly, Jill, I'm just surprised you're only smoking tobacco. But I didn't come here for that. We need to talk. Something's going on with Mama."

"Like what?"

"I think she's losing it. When I got up this morning, she was parked in front of the house. She sat there for a long time, just staring up at the house."

"Then what happened?"

"Nothing happened. Daddy pulled into the driveway and she drove off. But later I saw her drive by every half hour or so, going real slow and, you know, staring."

"That *is* weird. She showed up at the flea market too. Maybe there's a full moon or something."

Amy sighs. "What's the moon got to do with it?"

Jill hunkers down and leans against the side of the shed. "People get strange when there's a full moon."

Amy snorts. "You sound like some weirded-out hippie when you talk like that."

Jill takes in her twin's shiny blond bob, the fingernails filed into perfect pink ovals. "Oh, yeah," she says, jamming her own wood-stained hands into her pockets. "That shows how much you know. Grandy's a nurse and she says they always get their strangest cases when the moon's full."

Amy rolls her eyes. "Well, full moon, half moon, or no moon at all, Mama's getting stranger by the minute. It'd be just like her to do something trashy, like getting herself committed, before I go off to school."

Jill grinds her cigarette into the dirt. "Well, maybe you'll get lucky. Maybe she'll hold off going crazy until it's a more convenient time for you."

"Shut up."

"You shut up. I'm mad at Mama too, but that was a rotten thing to say."

"I don't care," Amy says, staring off into the distance. "I hate it here. I've always hated it. And now all this with Mama. I just want to leave before something else happens."

Jill swallows hard. "You know," she says, "maybe you're right. Maybe it is time for you to move on."

24

Betty

....

It's been a sixteen-hour day on the Alzheimer's Unit. Betty had clocked in before the sun came up and clocked out long after dark. She worked her own shift, then filled in for Dot Skurlock, who had covered for her during the beach weekend.

Betty has always been in good shape, but as she crosses the parking lot to her car she feels every second of her fifty-six years. She's muscle-aching, mind-numbing, eyes-welling tired. All she can think of is getting home and soaking in the tub. But when she gets to her car she remembers that she hadn't stopped for gas all weekend and the gas gauge is registering under a quarter of a tank. All she wants to do is lay her head on the steering wheel and bawl. How could she have broken her own rule of never letting the gauge get under half full?

She drives up East Main, then pulls into the Zippy Mart, next door to the Curl & Swirl. While she fills the gas tank, she stares across the parking lot at Maggie's apartment. The apartment is dark and Maggie's car is gone. It's strange not to know where her own daughter is and what she's doing. Until last spring they'd talked on the phone every day and were in and out of each other's houses several times a week. Maggie was always running errands for Mama Dean. She did their hair every Friday. Sometimes she'd just stop by with the girls and an invitation for Sunday dinner. When Betty shopped she bought dish towels and candles and baskets in pairs, one for herself and one for Maggie. She'd stop by to drop off coupons or cough medicine and end up staying to pin up a hem or have a cup of coffee. Over the years they'd had thousands of talks over endless cups of coffee.

Then one day, everything changed. And even though that was weeks ago, she still couldn't wrap her mind around the fact that if she stopped by the old house on Morehead, Maggie wouldn't be there. If she called the old phone number, it wouldn't be Maggie who answered.

A car blaring rap music pulls into the parking lot, jerking Betty back to the present. She goes inside the store to pay for the gas, then drives the five miles home. But when she rounds the corner onto Magnolia Street, she sees a tan Honda parked on the street. Is it just her imagination or is that really Maggie's car parked in front of her house? Then she sees the pale profile, the shock of dark hair. She dims her headlights and slows the car, afraid that any sudden move will scare off her daughter. But before she can get there, the tan Honda drives off into the night.

Betty shakes her head as she pulls into the driveway. "Oh, Maggie. What are you thinking?" she murmurs.

In spite of being so tired, Betty tosses and turns all night. At six-thirty she finally gives up and drags herself to the kitchen to start the coffee. She dresses while it's brewing, then carries a mug outside to the picnic table, where she sits and stares into the distance.

At eight, she tiptoes into Jill's bedroom.

"Wake up, sugar," she whispers. "I've got something I have to take care of. I need you to drive Mama Dean to Sunday school and pick her up after church."

A few minutes later she's driving through town. She parks her car, crosses the parking lot, hesitates for a moment, then rings the bell. She sees the slats in the miniblinds part, then snap back into place, but it's several long seconds before Maggie, dressed in a robe and rumpled T-shirt, appears at the door.

"Mother?" she says."What are you doing here? I thought you'd be in church."

Betty takes in her daughter's thin, pale face, the dark circles under her eyes. "Some things are more important than church. I had to see if you're all right," she says.

"Well, for goodness' sake! I'm fine. Come on in. Sit down. I'll get us some coffee."

Betty sits in a green wooden rocking chair by the window and surveys the room. It's small and dark, and smells of stale cigarette smoke. Maggie's unmade bed is a tangle of sheets and pillows on a nubby tan couch which is flanked by two end tables with matching brown lamps. There's a door leading to the kitchen and another to the bathroom. Except for a scattering of candles, a framed snapshot of Maggie's daughters, and a bright poster of Mattisse's *Goldfish* tacked above the couch, the apartment's as impersonal as a motel.

From the kitchen, Betty hears water running, cupboards banging, then an odd fizzing sound as the scent of Lysol fills the room. She knows Maggie's been smoking, but decides not to say anything.

With all that's on her mind it's important to choose her battles.

A moment later, Maggie carries two coffee mugs into the room, sets them on coasters on the coffee table, then begins tidying up. She folds and stacks the pillow and sheets on the closet shelf, opens the miniblinds, and finally perches on the edge of the couch.

"This is the first time you've been here, isn't it? I know it's a mess, but what do you think?"

Betty glances around the room, her gaze coming to rest on her daughter. "I didn't come to see your apartment. We need to talk."

Maggie sighs, then stares into her mug. "What do you want to talk about?"

"I saw you last night."

"Oh, that," she says. "That was the darnedest thing. I was driving around and all of a sudden I realized I was on your street."

Betty crosses the room and sits on the couch next to her daughter. "Come on, Maggie," she says softly. "I saw you. You were parked in front of the house."

Maggie looks at her mother, then looks away. "So! I didn't do anything wrong."

"I didn't say you did. But when you took off like that I got worried."

There's a moment of thick silence, then Maggie says, "I'm sorry, Mama. But, you don't know what it's like not to see your own children. Sometimes I drive by, hoping to catch a glimpse of them because I don't know what else to do . . ." She tries to go on, but her lips tremble.

Betty feels a flash of annoyance. "For goodness' sakes, Maggie. You've got to bite the bullet. If you want to see the girls, you have to face Steven and Mama Dean."

Maggie slumps. "I can't."

"I don't get it. So what if you and Mama Dean have a fight. You've been fighting and making up your whole life. Why is this time so different?"

Maggie's eyes flash. "Of course you don't get it! You've always been so cool and collected."

Betty is stunned. "You've got to be kidding. When I left your daddy and brought you back here, I was terrified. Back then, divorce was a scandal. Divorced women were an even bigger scandal. I got a job, kept my head down, tried to raise you and go on about my business. Then one day you came running to me screaming. You'd overheard Mama Dean tell a neighbor that your daddy was dead."

"She's so weird. Why would she say a thing like that?"

Betty shrugs. "I don't know. I guess she thought death was more fitting than divorce, that if I was a widow people would feel sorry for me instead of thinking I was no-account. But you were only four and you believed her, believed your daddy really was dead. Well, that flew all over me, so I carried you from house to house and told everyone the truth. And you know what? Mama Dean had a fit that lasted a week. But as bad as it was, we both lived right through it."

They sit in silence for a while. Finally, Maggie says, "I know you're trying to make me feel better, but there's so much you don't know. . . ." Then fat, salty tears are running down her face onto her T-shirt.

Betty puts her arms around her. "Oh, sugar, I do know. I've known for months."

Maggie's eyes are wide. "Mother?"

"I saw a pickup with an out-of-state license parked behind your apartment and I knew it was Jerry Roberts."

Maggie gulps for air. "I wanted to tell you, but I was afraid you'd think I was a heathen."

"Well, I was shook up for a while. But you know how it is with mothers and daughters. You can be mad enough to shake them, but mostly you think, oh, no, my little girl's in trouble, what'll I do?"

Betty pulls away and looks into Maggie's eyes. "Is that what's going on? You feeling like a heathen? Is that why you've avoided everyone all these months?"

Maggie wipes her eyes with the backs of her hands and nods. "We didn't mean for it to happen. And then when it did, I didn't know how to tell you. After I left Steven, I went to see you, but you were so shocked and torn up . . . and Mama Dean . . . she always expected the worst from me . . ." Maggie takes a deep breath and pauses. "Oh, Lord, I know I'm going on and on, but it's such a relief to talk about it."

Betty pats Maggie's hand. It's so small she swears she can feel all the bones in it.

Maggie leans into the couch and closes her eyes for a moment. "I don't know about you, but I didn't sleep all night. I need some more coffee and a couple of aspirins."

When she returns from the kitchen, she's carrying their refilled mugs and bottle of aspirin. She hands Betty two tablets and takes two herself.

"It's a mess, isn't it? Jerry said it'd be a mess for a while, but I never expected all this."

"You really love him, don't you."

Maggie's face is soft, her eyes shining. "Oh, Mama, he's great. I know you met him when we were kids, but I can't wait 'til you meet him now. You'll see. I should have married him in the first place, but then I wouldn't have had my girls, would I?" She pauses, takes a sip of her coffee. "So what do you think? Do you think they'll ever accept all this, accept Jerry?

"It'll take time, Maggie. There's a lot to take in."

Maggie sighs. "I know. I've already waited twenty years. I was just thinking about what Mama Dean did the first time she met Jerry back in high school. She called you at work and shouted into the phone, "Get home, Betty. A wolf in sheep's clothing is fixing to carry off our baby."

"Lord, honey, we didn't know what to think. He wore tight jeans, had a pack of cigarettes rolled up in the sleeve of his T-shirt. And that car, with the mufflers roaring . . . we thought he was fast. Some kind of an outlaw or something."

"Oh, Mama, back then a boy had to act like an outlaw, especially if he was a poet."

Betty smiles. "I never thought about that. But you're right. The first time Mama Dean met Charlie, she said, 'I guess you know he's some kind of foreigner.' As if I hadn't noticed he had an accent."

"You're still seeing him, then?"

Betty smiles again and nods.

For a while, both of them are lost in their own thoughts. Finally, Maggie says, "Do you remember when Mama Dean met Steven? She said, 'That Steven Presson's a man to go to the well with. Why, anyone who can't get along with him, couldn't get along with Jesus Christ.'"

For the first time that morning, Betty laughs. "That's Mama Dean all right! She was thrilled because he had a full-time job and he'd brought her a Whitman's Sampler."

They both laugh.

Betty sets her mug on the coffee table. "That reminds me. You'll never guess what happened. Steven called Mama Dean a couple of weeks ago and they had a big fight."

"Really?"

"I guess he accused her of something and she said she wasn't putting up with his S.B. anymore."

"S.B.?"

"She always calls B.S. S.B. She must get it mixed up with S.O.B. or something."

"Mama Dean cursed?"

"I reckon she did. She said she'd defended him all over hell and half of Georgia, but now he could kiss her foot. Then she got twice as mad because he'd caused her to curse on a Sunday. But you know what? I was just thinking . . . this might be a good time to hightail it over there and start wearing her down. Take her an Impossible Pie. You know how she loves your Impossible Pie. And do it soon, honey, do it while she's still mad at Steven, but before some old gossip tells her about Jerry."

It's a little after ten when Betty leaves Maggie's apartment. There's still plenty of time to go home and take Mama Dean to church. But she isn't ready to go home yet. She needs to be by herself, to breathe fresh air and think things over. She drives down Townsend Avenue, past the city limits sign, the That'lldu Bar and Grill, the farmer's market, then under a bridge painted with the warning JESUS OR HELL. Within seconds she sees cattle grazing near hillsides so layered with kudzu they look like dusty, green mountains. She passes the old Dingler farmhouse, then pulls off the paved highway, onto the unmarked dirt road that leads to Belews Pond.

She parks the car and gets out. The parking area is a weedy patch of deep rutted tire tracks littered with beer and soft drink cans, fast-food wrappers, and cigarette butts. Betty sighs. She hasn't been out this way in years. And except for these vandals, neither has anyone else.

For a moment she considers getting back in her car and leaving. Instead, she takes a deep breath, climbs up the rise to the woods, and starts picking her way along an overgrown trail. The path is narrower than she remembers, tangled with underbrush and roots in unexpected places. She watches her feet, holds her arms in front of her to keep from getting smacked in the face with briars and branches. She's so busy concentrating that it's a surprise when she steps out into a clearing. She stands there for a moment, watching a hawk swoop low. Then she crosses the field to the pond.

She sits near the bank under a small stand of shade trees and kicks off her sneakers. Then she stares off into the distance and thinks about secrets. Maggie's secret. Her own. Only this morning, she'd been sure that Maggie was coming apart. But after they'd talked, and Maggie's secret came out, they'd both been giddy with relief. Maybe confession really was good for the soul.

Now Betty wonders how different her life would be if she hadn't spent so much time hiding her own past. She'd told Maggie most of how it had been with her. But she hadn't told her everything. How could she? How did you go about telling a secret you'd kept for thirty-eight years?

Maggie said she should have married Jerry in the first place. Now Betty wonders if they'd be married and happy right now if she hadn't panicked and interfered all those years ago.

She remembers every detail of that day. Maggie's graduation.

Her father's surprise visit. Then the stunning announcement that Maggie would be moving to Chapel Hill with him. He'd found her a summer job and signed her up for beauty school in the fall. They'd be leaving in an hour. Maggie's life had been decided.

She can still see the girl's confusion, the look in her eyes that said, "Daddy's only fooling, right?" She remembers how she'd avoided those eyes and hardened her heart to the tears, as she and Mama Dean went upstairs to pack Maggie's suitcase.

Betty still squirms when she thinks about it. But she hadn't known what else to do after Mama Dean read Maggie's diary, then shown it to her. She'd scolded Mama Dean, told her to put the diary away and leave Maggie alone. But then she saw the fear and worry in her mother's eyes and she knew it was her fault. Her fault her mother was so hard on Maggie. Her fault Mama Dean listened in on the girl's phone calls and followed her everywhere. So she'd read the page, and Mama Dean's suspicions and her own worst fears were confirmed. In her small, cramped penmanship, Maggie had written that on graduation night she planned to "do it" with Jerry Roberts.

That's when her own past rushed in, nearly drowning her. She was seventeen when she and Annie moved to Raleigh for nursing school. Two young girls away from home for the first time, looking for excitement. A year later, after she'd graduated from LPN school, she'd met Smiling Jack Sweet at a party. Jack's nickname suited him. He was dark and handsome, with a dangerous Rhett Butler smile. She watched him from a distance. He was the best-looking man she'd ever seen and she was sure he'd never notice her. When he asked her to dance she was so surprised she actually looked behind her thinking he was talking to someone else. But before the party was over, he asked for her phone number and soon they were inseparable. Sometimes he took her dancing or to a movie. But mostly they'd go for walks or just drive around Raleigh. The day he told her he loved her she couldn't believed it. Jack, who could have anyone he wanted, had chosen her.

But six months later, when she told him she was pregnant, he went pale and vanished from her life. She remembers the sleepless nights when she walked the floor and cried.

Mama Dean had told her all men were alike. They were only after one thing and they'd say anything to get it. If she got carried away, he'd lose respect for her. He'd brag all over town and her reputation would be ruined. She'd wind up alone, maybe pregnant or worse. It was her fault if things went too far. Her responsibility to keep her feelings in check and her knees together. Men were animals. They couldn't be expected to control themselves.

But Jack said he loved her. She thought he was different. How could she have been such a fool?

She remembers waking in a cold sweat, crying. She'd dreamed the hospital where she worked found out she was pregnant and notified Mama Dean. She'd been sent to a home for unwed mothers where they told her she'd be selfish to keep the baby. Hadn't she already proven she was wayward? A girl like that had nothing to offer a baby. The right thing to do, the only thing to do was to let a childless, God-fearing, church-going couple adopt it.

Then, one day, as suddenly as he'd disappeared, Jack was back. He said he was sorry. He said he still loved her. When they held on to each other and cried, it was the first time she realized Jack was just a boy and as scared as she was. After a quick justice-of-the-peace wedding, Jack told her that during the weeks he'd disappeared he'd enlisted in the Army. Three weeks later he left for Fort Bragg, then Korea.

She wrote home that she was married, but lied about the date. When she started to show, she bound her breasts and wore tight girdles so she could squeeze herself into her uniforms. Because along with her shame, in 1947 being pregnant was grounds for dismissal at the hospital.

It was only at night, after her shift was over that she allowed herself to linger over Jack's letters and dream about their life together or she'd rest her hands on her belly and wonder at the new life stirring inside her.

But then came the day Mama Dean surprised her by coming to Raleigh on a Greyhound. She'd never forget the look on her mother's face when she'd had to say the words, "Oh, Mama, I'm sorry. Oh, Mama, I'm going to have a baby."

Even now, thirty-eight years later, her face burns with shame when she thinks about it. But Maggie was an adult now. Maybe she had the right to know. Maybe it would help her sort through the confusion of her life. Would she understand why Mama Dean had watched her like a hawk? Why they'd read her diary then shipped her off to live with her daddy all those years ago? Betty sighs. She'd carried this burden for so long maybe confession would be good for *her* soul.

But it was more complicated than that. Did Maggie need to know that when Jack came home from Korea he was a stranger? That he stayed silent for hours, staring straight ahead, as distant from her and the baby, as if he were still thousands of miles away. Every night after supper, he'd leave the apartment to go out with his friends and return hours later, knee-walking drunk.

Betty was only twenty-two. She'd never felt so scared and helpless in her life. She did everything she could think of to try to win him back. She cooked his favorite meals and kept herself and the little apartment as neat and pretty as possible. She took Annie's advice and bought perfume and a black silky nightie and tried not to feel hurt and humiliated when he turned away from her at night. She tried setting Maggie, fresh and sweet from her bath, on his lap, hoping the baby would touch him in a way she never could. But no matter what she did nothing ever changed.

Within weeks she was sure Mama Dean was right. Jack felt trapped and resentful. He'd never forgive her for forcing him into marriage and he'd punish her with his silence and drinking for the rest of her days. She'd fallen in love and it had been her undoing.

After Annie left Raleigh to marry Ed, Betty had no one to turn to, so she took Maggie and moved back to Poplar Grove.

This was years before Vietnam, long before anyone ever heard of Post Traumatic Stress Syndrome. Later, Betty wondered if that's what happened to Jack. Because after their divorce, twice a month, as regular as clockwork, he made the two-hour trip to Poplar Grove to see Maggie. His eyes were sad, his voice was soft and apologetic, and instead of alcohol, he smelled of Aqua Velva, Wrigley's chewing gum, and Chesterfields. But it was too late. When he came to see Maggie, Betty never let her guard down.

One Sunday night, she was waiting for them in the kitchen. As they climbed the back porch steps, she'd heard him say to Maggie, "See ya around, fart-blossom," his voice all gruff and casual-like. It had flown all over her. But when she'd opened the door to pull Maggie inside, she'd seen there were tears in his eyes.

He still changed jobs too often and would probably never grow up, but he was a good father to Maggie and the child adored him.

Betty tried to hold her head high and get on with her life. But she spent the next few years waiting to be exposed. As if the words "had to get married" were written all over her in indelible ink. As if any minute the whispers would start, "That's Betty Sweet. I knew her in Raleigh. She had to get married, you know."

At first her co-workers invited her to take in a movie or stop off for coffee after their shifts were over, but she made polite excuses and went straight home to Maggie and Mama Dean. Eventually they stopped asking. Annie had said, "Why are you punishing yourself? Don't you think you *deserve* fun and friends?" Now she wonders if Annie had been right. Maybe she didn't think she deserved it. Or maybe she'd been hiding behind Maggie and Mama Dean because somewhere deep inside she believed it was safer than going out, safer then risking the possibility of meeting someone new, of opening her heart and having it broken again.

She'd been her own judge and jury and given herself a lifetime sentence of solitary confinement. But now she'd met Charlie and she longed to have that sentence commuted.

She gets up stiffly, and walks to the edge of the pond. She can see the bright blue sky, a stand of loblolly pines, and her own reflection. Opalescent dragonflies zip low, then hover over the reeds. A moment later she looks skyward as the hawk sweeps low, dipping its wings.

No. She'd never tell Maggie. Who would it help after all these years? But it was time to forgive herself. Time to move on. It was a sin really, a sin against God the way she'd stunted her life.

25

Maggie

After her mother leaves, Maggie showers and dresses, then grabs her car keys and heads out the door.

A few minutes later she turns onto Chatham Road toward the farmhouse and sees Jerry riding his John Deere half an acre away. She waves, pulls into the driveway, and hides the car behind an outbuilding. By the time she gets out, Jerry is by her side, giving her a quick, sweaty kiss.

"What's up?" he says, smiling into her eyes.

She grins and squeezes his hand. "Let's go inside. I've got something to tell you." They are barely in the kitchen when she throws her arms around him. "I told her! Mother came over this morning and I told her about us. Oh, Jerry, I did it! I can't believe it, but I finally actually did it!"

"Oh, honey, that's great! I've never been so glad to hear anything in my life," he says, lifting her off her feet and whirling her around. Then he sits at the kitchen table and pulls her onto his lap. "Tell me what happened. I want to know everything."

"I started to tell her, but I couldn't go through with it. Then, all at once she was filling in the blanks. Turns out she's known for months. Oh, Jerry, it's going to be all right. She knows and she hasn't disowned me. Now we have to make an Impossible Pie for Mama Dean."

Jerry laughs. "Slow down, honey. You're making my head spin. What did you say about Mama Dean?"

"Mother reminded me about this pie I used to make. Mama Dean's favorite. I figure it's as good a way as any to get started. I'll bribe her with pies, do her hair, whatever she wants. And even if she fusses at me I'll just keep doing it until I wear her down."

"You think it'll work?"

"It beats what I've been doing. Avoiding everyone. Feeling like homemade sin . . ."

Jerry smiles. "You really think you can buy her off?"

"Did I ever tell you the story about the Whitman Sampler?"

He kisses her long and deep. "You're a nut. Did I ever tell you I love you to pieces?"

"Yeah, but tell me again," she says, resting her head on his chest. "Let's go to bed?"

"Oh, honey. Not now. I'm on a roll with this pie thing."

"All right," he says. He stands up and opens a cupboard door. "I've got the fixin's for all kinds of pie. Key Lime, Mississippi Mud, Chocolate Silk . . . ."

Jerry with his well-stocked, everything-in-its-place kitchen, always cooked for them, marinated steaks, blackened fish, spices and desserts with such exotic names she couldn't pronounce them.

She laughs. "Do you have any Bisquick?"

He looks puzzled. "You mean pancake mix?"

"I use it for Impossible Pie. Mama Dean's favorite's Impossible Pie."

Jerry grins. "Why doesn't that surprise me?"

She punches him playfully, then reads aloud the recipe on the back of the box while he measures the ingredients into separate containers. "Now what?" he says.

"You dump it all in a bowl and mix it all together."

His eyes are wide. "That can't be right. What about the crust? What about keeping the wet and dry ingredients separate?"

Maggie grins. "Sometimes you just have to throw caution to the wind and mix the wet and the dry together."

Jerry just looks at her.

"It's all right, honey," she says. "It makes its own crust. That's why they call it Impossible Pie."

He's still shaking his head and frowning as he mixes everything together, then pours the batter into a pan. When he looks up, she's grinning. "You're enjoying this, aren't you?"

She reaches up and kisses him on the chin. "I was just thinking how lucky I am. Even when something sounds crazy you go along with me."

He holds her close. "Oh, yeah?"

"Yeah," she says, nuzzling his neck.

"Well, I've got a crazy idea I'd like to explore."

"Uh-huh. Well, then, why don't we set the timer for fifty-five minutes and see what we can come up with."

Maggie spends the day repeating her mother's words: "Mama Dean had a fit, but we both lived through it. Mama Dean had a fit, but we both lived through it." She says it over and over like a mantra. Later, while she and Jerry wait for the Impossible Pie to cool, she dances around the kitchen to her own rap song version. "Mama Dean had a fit, uh-huh, uh-huh. Mama Dean had a fit and we lived right through it. Uh-huh, uh-huh!"

But, as she drives toward the boardinghouse, with the Impossible Pie resting on the passenger seat, the words become a prayer. "Please, God, please. I'll never ask for another thing, if you'll let us both live through it."

She turns the corner onto Magnolia, then panics and speeds past the house. She's dizzy and sweating and gripping the steering wheel so tightly it's a wonder it doesn't snap off in her hands. She pulls over at the Zippy Mart, rolls down the window, and breathes a little. Then she turns the key in the ignition and sets off toward the outskirts of town. Maybe a nice ride in the country will calm her nerves, give her time to think of what she'll say to Mama Dean.

A half hour later, she drives past the house again. This time her mother's car is parked in the driveway. But instead of feeling reassured, her mother's presence throws her completely. Her sweet little mama, who somehow still believes in her, is expecting her. What will her mother think if she doesn't go through with it? How will she feel about having a sniveling coward for a daughter? Oh, Lord! Disappointing her mother is almost as bad as facing Mama Dean.

She speeds past the house again and thinks about what Jerry said. "She can't kill you. She can't even send you to Vietnam." So, what was it about Mama Dean that was so terrifying? So what if she yells? She'd been yelling her whole life. But that was the thing. Mama Dean *had* been yelling her whole life. Going on and on, never letting anything go, never letting up until everyone around her was so miserable they never wanted to go against her again. All Maggie had ever wanted was to make her grandmother proud. But no matter how hard she tried, Mama Dean always looked at her like she was responsible for the world.

Well, she is sick of it. Sick of feeling like pure crud! She feels a surge of adrenaline and steps on the gas. Her courage is high. She'll face Mama Dean, have it out with her once and for all. She is speeding along Main Street when a truck pulls out in front of her, forcing her to swerve and slam on her brakes.

"Moron," she shouts, as she blows the horn, and flips off the driver.

She can't believe it! She's never done anything like that before.

The truck driver pumps his brakes, then sticks his head out the window and shakes his fist. Oh Lord! What if he forces her off the road and jerks her out of her car? It happens every day. She's seen it on the eleven o'clock news. If she wound up in the hospital, delivering an Impossible Pie, maybe then Mama Dean would be sorry.

She makes a sharp right onto Broad Street and the truck keeps going. All she wants to do is put her head on the steering wheel and cry, especially when she sees that the pie has shifted. Now her peace offering looks for all the world like a coconut-crumb cake. She moans, but presses on, circling back to Main Street, then Magnolia again. This time she slows down and stares at the house. It's six o'clock. There's a light on in the kitchen. For as long as she can remember, Mother and Mama Dean have always had supper at six o'clock. Sundays meant pot roast, cooked with potatoes and carrots in Lipton's Onion soup mix, one week; fried chicken, mashed potatoes, and snap beans the next.

Just thinking about them sitting in that dark, cozy kitchen

makes her feel sick with longing. But what if the shock of suddenly seeing her, pushes Mama Dean over the edge? What if she doesn't live right through it? How would it feel to spend the rest of her life knowing she'd killed her own grandmother.

"Stop scaring yourself," she mutters. "You've got to go through with it. Even if it kills you. Even if it kills her."

She drives to the end of the block, parks the car at the corner, and gets out. She keeps her head down, hugging the pie against her chest, hoping no one will spot her. She hurries past Blackburn's Electric, Benfield's Alterations, and the old Hatley place, which is being torn down for a Texaco station.

She looks around, then darts up the steps to the house. Her stomach feels punched and her heart is beating harder than when the truck nearly hit her.

She takes a deep breath and rings the doorbell. Her mother answers, looks around nervously, then leads her back to the kitchen.

"Mama," she says. "Maggie's come to see you. She's brought an Impossible Pie."

Mama Dean's face goes white and she bites her lip.

"Oh, Law. Oh, no," she wails. Then she looks around wildly, pushes herself up from the table and zigzags down the hall toward her room.

Maggie feels the room swirl around her. "Mama Dean," she calls, as she starts down the hall on bloodless legs. "Mama Dean, please, talk to me. Oh, Mama Dean, I'm sorry."

26

Jill

....

Jill lies on her bed staring at the ceiling. It was hard to believe that only this morning she'd been happy. She and Freedom had discovered a flea market in Charlotte with acres of buildings and tents filled with antiques, collectibles, paintings, and wall hangings. Everything from fine art to primitive. The place was so crowded with customers, the girls could barely get through the aisles. And the vendors! The vendors were dressed in vintage clothes from the thirties and forties, some wore tie-dye and Birkenstocks with crocheted hats over dreadlocks, others dressed Willie Nelson–style in bib overalls, fat braids, and bandannas.

They spent several thrilling minutes following a man from the art-deco building who wore a full leather biker outfit, cap and all, along with thick black eyeliner.

"Lord, Freedom, I feel like I died and went to New York City!"

Freedom grins and nods. "I know. The dealers look like us and there's not a country goose in sight. And check out the customers. They're paying money hand over fist and for anything original. Just think what they'll pay for Jill's Chainsaw Art! Come on. Let's go see what a table rents for, then I'll treat you to a bagel or Perrier, something New Yorkish."

They drift off toward the manager's office and as if by some silent signal they slide their sunglasses over their eyes and sing in unison, "My future's so bright I need to wear shades. Future's so bright I need to wear shades."

Jill buries her face in the pillow and moans. Had she been smug for a moment? Had she jinxed herself by being too happy? Because just when it looked like things were coming together everything fell apart.

They were sitting at a table in the food court when it happened. Freedom stared past her and hissed. "Don't move, Jill, it's your dad!"

"No shit!

"Oh, Jill, don't look!"

But it was too late. Jill had already spun around in her chair.

It was her father all right. Her father and Theo Bloodworth. They were holding hands and laughing, and her father was looking into Mrs. Bloodworth's eyes in a way he'd never looked at her mother.

Suddenly there was nothing Jill wanted more than to be at Grandy's and Mama Dean's, alone, in her room.

"It doesn't prove anything," Freedom had said in the van on the way home. "Maybe Mrs. Bloodworth stumbled and he grabbed her to keep her from falling. Maybe they just bumped into each other and it just looked like they were holding hands."

Jill didn't want to talk about it. She just stared out the van window and thought about all the years her father and Mrs. Bloodworth had gone to all those cheesy commitee meetings together—meetings that lasted late into the night—entire weekends spent tombstone rubbing. She remembers her graduation party. Her father had stood around like the Lord of the Manor while her mother, dressed in a faded shirtwaist, darted everywhere, setting up tables, fixing and serving food. She remembers being embarrassed because her mother reminded her, for all the world, of Edith Bunker. While all this was going on, her father followed Mrs. Bloodworth everywhere and hung on her every word. Later, when Mrs. Bloodworth made a fuss over Jill's wood carvings, her father had gathered everyone into the dining room and announced that he was sending Jill to art school. She'd been so thrilled she had cried. But her father was only showing off for Mrs. Bloodworth.

The minute Freedom pulls into the driveway, Jill gets out of the van, runs to her room, and flops on the bed. All she wants is to be alone and quiet. But she can hear Grandy and Mama Dean arguing through the air vent. Something about her mother and an Impossible Pie.

Jesus. Parents. Her mother was pathetic and her father was an ass.

That's when the whole sorry day catches up with her and she starts to cry. She gets up, crosses the room, and covers the air vent with her pillow. Then she climbs back into bed and pulls the blanket up over her head.

AUGUST 1985

27

Maggie

....

At first, every time the Curl & Swirl's door opened, Maggie's heart pounded. She kept expecting to see Steven, her daughters, Steven's mother, Mama Dean, Preacher Poteat, and the entire Gladys Spivey crowd. They would close in on her, shake their fingers in her face, and call her unspeakable names. They'd do it when the shop was its busiest and all the customers would witness her shame. Then they'd drag her out on Main Street and while the whole town watched, they'd hold her down and paint a red letter A on her forehead.

Then she'd realize the person coming through the door was only a beauty supply salesman, UPS, or one of their regular customers. But it always took several long minutes for her heartbeat to return to normal.

So far, the only one who'd appeared from her worst-case-scenario daymare was the town gossip, Gladys Spivey, who had a standing appointment with Shirley every Saturday. Maggie nearly fainted the first time she saw her, but now weeks had gone by and Miss Spivey hadn't looked at her, much less spoken. She just sat under Shirley's dryer, with her arms folded over her chest, wearing a face as pinched as if her underwear were on backward.

Maggie doesn't realize she's gripping the edge of the picnic table until Jerry pats her hand. "Where did you drift off to?" he asks, refilling her coffee mug.

She smiles. "I *was* drifting. You just saved me from work on my day off."

He fills his own mug. "But I thought you liked your job."

"I do. Well, mostly, I do. Except for Gladys Spivey day."

"You can't worry about what she says."

She sighs. "Yeah, my plate's already full what with my family and friends not speaking to me."

He sips his coffee and stares off into the distance. "I've been meaning to tell you, Mary Price called last night. She and Hoyt are having a cookout Sunday. They've invited a bunch of our old high school friends. They want us to come."

Her stomach lurches.

He looks at her, then looks away. "We said we'd start going places, remember? We'd just go separately then blend in with the crowd. Sneak up on them gradually until everyone accepts us as a couple."

Tears spring to her eyes and she stares into her mug. "Oh, Lord."

"It'll be all right, Maggie. That's what we did at the class reunion and it all worked out. We've got to show up, keep showing up, or we'll never make any headway."

Her voice is low. "I can't."

"You can't or you won't?"

"I can't hardly breathe just thinking about it."

There's an edge in his voice. "So when do you think you'll *be* ready? The longer we wait the harder it'll get."

"Lord, Jerry, don't push me. Not now."

"I don't mean to push . . . it's just . . . oh, never mind." He lets go of her hand, picks up their mugs, and goes into the house.

She follows him into the kitchen. He keeps his back to her as he jams the mugs into the dishwasher and slams the door.

Tears gather behind her eyes. "Don't be mad."

"I'm not mad . . . it's just . . . we knew it wouldn't be easy. Why do you have to make everything harder than it has to be?"

She's stung. "I don't mean to . . . Oh, Lord. You don't know how I feel!"

"Then tell me."

"I have told you! I've been telling you all week. Why can't you understand how awful it was with Mama Dean?" She tries to go on, but tears fill her eyes and she looks away.

"How could I *not* know. That's all you talked about. You've got to stop dwelling on it. It's over." He reaches for her hand, but she stiffens and pulls away.

"It's just a cookout—a few old friends milling around Mary Price's backyard, eating burgers, tossing a Frisbee. If we keep hiding out, we'll be back to square one."

"But I *am* back to square one. Lord, Jerry. Don't you get it? If my own grandmother won't speak to me, everyone else must think . . . how can I face them when I know what they're thinking?"

His voice is hoarse. "But you don't know what they're thinking. Maybe they're avoiding you because you're avoiding them."

She crosses the room and stares out the kitchen window. Her voice is trembling. "I thought you, of all people, would understand."

"I've tried. Lord knows, I've tried. But I'm running out of patience. I want us to be a couple, to walk through town holding hands, but that's never going to happen if you won't . . ." He rakes his hands through his hair, takes a deep breath. "I keep thinking about why we broke up back in high school. You couldn't stand up for yourself then. You won't stand up for yourself now. We've had a second chance. Don't you see how lucky we are?"

She nods, but she can't seem to stop her tears.

He looks past her, out the window. "But maybe you don't care about that . . . maybe this is too hard for you."

"How can you think that?" she shouts.

His eyes flash. "What am I supposed to think? Tell me, Maggie, are you sorry you gave up your old safe life? Are you ashamed of *us?*"

He crosses the kitchen and goes out the back door, slamming it behind him. A moment later she hears the sound of his truck's engine, then gravel flying.

She stumbles to the kitchen table and sinks into a chair. Oh, Lord. What if this is it? What if after all they've been through, it's over? Nothing had changed since high school. She'd lost him then, she was losing him now.

Why couldn't he understand that she wasn't trying to make it harder? She *had* seen their friends. Modine and Doris, Geneva and Jessie Rae were always passing the Curl & Swirl with their shopping or on their way to lunch at Millie's Percolator Grill. Sometimes they'd stand outside the shop, talking and laughing, saying their good-byes. She'd waved to them a few times. She'd even considered going outside to visit between customers. But after her visit to Mama Dean everything had changed. Now when she saw her old friends, her ears roared and her heart pounded. She'd dart to the back of the shop and cower there, until she was sure they were gone or Shirley came looking for her.

She gets up from the table, opens a cupboard door, then slams it shut, opens another, and slams it. Then she stomps down the hall to the bedroom where they'd made love all these months. She picks up a pillow and throws it across the room, picks up the other pillow and pounds it with her fists.

"Dammit, Jerry! Can't you see I'm doing my best!" she yells. Then she throws herself across the bed and cries.

Later, when she's all cried out, she rolls onto her back and stares at the ceiling. The bed is wide and empty. She's never felt so alone in her life. She thinks about how sad and empty her life had been without him, how she'd spent most of it sleepwalking. Oh, Lord. All in the world she wants is for Jerry to be lying here beside her. That's when it hits her. Whatever happened, he was the center of her life. But she *was* doing what she'd done back in school. She was giving him up. Letting guilt and fear and other people come between them. There wasn't much else she could have done back then, but she wasn't a helpless schoolgirl anymore. Jerry had warned her it would be a mess. But every time it got messy, instead of pulling herself together, she fell apart.

That day with Mama Dean *had* been awful. But what had she expected? She'd avoided Mama Dean for months, then she'd gone barreling over there, like a hit-and-run driver, thinking an Impossible Pie would fix everything. No wonder Mama Dean had gone all to pieces. It was a wonder she hadn't had a heart attack.

What was it her mother had said? "Mama Dean had a fit that lasted all week, but we lived right through it."

Well, maybe Mama Dean *needed* to have a fit that lasted a week. Maybe Maggie should have gone back, kept going back for a week or however long it took for Mama Dean to tell her off, pitch her fit and get it over with. If she'd gone back, kept going back, maybe things would be settled right now.

So what if it was messy and scary and complicated. None of that mattered. Jerry had moved from Florida to Poplar Grove, uprooted his whole life for her. But when he'd asked her to go to a simple cookout she got all torn up, wallowed in guilt and self-pity, acted like a child. No wonder he thought she longed for her old safe life. That she didn't want him enough. That she was ashamed of *them*.

Oh, Lord. When she thinks about life without him she feels bleak and hopeless and filled with regret.

Maggie wipes her eyes with her fists, rolls onto her stomach, and props herself up on her elbows. If she doesn't pull herself together she'll lose him, then spend the rest of her life alone, knowing it was her fault.

She gets up, goes into the bathroom and splashes her face with water, finds her purse, and dabs on a little makeup. She straightens the pillows, smoothes the bedspread. Then she takes a deep breath, goes to the kitchen, and calls Mary Price.

She has just hung up the phone when she hears the sounds of an engine and gravel crunching in the driveway.

She meets him at the door. For a moment they just stand there. Then she puts her arms around him. "Oh, Jerry, I'm sorry. I never want you to think you're not worth it, that *we're* not worth it. You mean everything to me."

For a while they just stand there holding on to each other. Finally Maggie says, "I called Mary Price. I told her we'd take banana pudding to the cookout."

"What?"

"Unless you don't want to take banana pud—"

"Wait a minute. You've got my head spinning. Are you saying you *are* going to the cookout?"

She nods. "If you still want me to."

"But I thought . . . you said . . ."

She gazes into his eyes. "I know. But I *do* know how lucky I am. I want us to be a couple, to walk down the street holding hands, too. Oh, honey, I'm still scared about facing all those people. But you're right. I've got to go to the cookout or I'll never work up the courage to tackle Mama Dean again."

Saturday afternoon, just before closing, Maggie is cleaning up her section and talking about the day when Modine Dingler, Doris Binfield, and Jessie Rae Moore come into the shop.

Maggie's heart beats wildly under her smock. It's her worst-case-scenario daymare, but instead of her enemies cornering her in the shop, it's her old high school friends.

Shirley, who is sweeping hair into a pile, looks up. "Sorry, ladies. We're fixing to close."

"We're not here to get our hair done," Modine says.

"It's just . . . well, we've come to talk to Maggie," Doris stammers.

"We just decided this whole . . . uh . . . situation's gone on too long."

Shirley, Dixie, and Lurleen stop doing what they're doing. They stare at Maggie and the women, the women and Maggie. The shop is silent, then Maggie hears the faint sound of wind chimes as Mrs. Mabes, Shirley's mother, comes out of the back room carrying a stack of clean folded towels. She gives the wind chimes a look that should freeze them into silence forever.

Mrs. Mabes is eighty-three and weighs about eighty-three pounds, but even when she's not doing anything her eyes dart, her head bobs, and her feet tap. Folks around town give her a wide berth and whisper stories about people who "spontaneous combust."

The women stare at their feet. "Hey, Mrs. Mabes," they chorus shrilly.

"They've come to see Maggie, Mama. Maggie, do want us to give you a little privacy?"

Perspiration trickles down Maggie sides, but before she can answer, Mrs. Mabes narrows her eyes. "Is this about to get ugly?"

"Ma'am?" they say, their eyes wide.

Shirley puts her hands on hips. "It won't get ugly. I don't allow ugly in my shop."

"Lord, Shirley, we didn't come here to cause any trouble. Maggie's our friend. At least *we* thought we were friends. But she left Steven without a word to any of us and now . . ." Doris's voice trembles and she ducks her head and fiddles with the hem of her T-shirt.

Modine interrupts. "And now it's been months and she still hasn't talked to us. I mean we've known each other since we were little bitty kids. If she never intends to speak to us again, the least she can do is tell us."

Mrs. Mabes makes an odd hissing sound.

"It's all right, Mrs. Mabes. I do need to talk to them." Maggie stares at her feet and her voice is faint. "I'm sorry, you all. I know I should have done this a long time ago, but the longer I waited . . ." Then Jerry floats into her mind and she takes a deep breath, straightens her shoulders and forces herself to look up. "I had to leave Steven. Things had been bad between us for so long, I just had

192

to. I'm sorry I've hurt a lot of people and I'd hate it if you all don't want to be friends anymore, but you need to know that no matter what happens, I'm never going back."

Nobody says anything for so long, Maggie is debating whether to throw herself at their mercy or make a run for the back door. Finally, Doris says, "And then . . ."

Maggie's face feels hot. "What do you mean 'and then'?"

Modine's eyes flash. "Honestly, Maggie," then, "Good grief! Did you think we came here to tell you to go back to Steven?"

"You mean you didn't?"

"Lord, no," they all say in unison.

"But then what . . ."

Doris concentrates on her sneakers. "The thing is, well, uh, the thing is, it's one thing for you to leave Steven, but we come here to see if you left us too?"

"I don't know what . . ."

"You never call . . ."

"You run off when you see . . ."

"But I thought . . ."

"Well, we thought . . ."

"I didn't know . . ."

"Good grief, you all," Modine shouts. "We'll never get anywhere if we keep pussyfooting around. What we're trying to say is you've been avoiding us for months . . ."

"But I thought you all were avoiding me."

"Oh, Maggie," Jessie Rae says. "I mean we all liked to have died when it first happened, what with you and Steven being together for so long."

"But we weren't avoiding you," Modine says.

"Bullshit and applesauce," Mrs. Mabes mutters.

Shirley pats her mother's arm. "Settle down, Mama! You're getting your bowels in an uproar."

Mrs. Mabes narrows her eyes. "All I can say is I know what I know."

"Well, maybe we were avoiding you," Modine says. "But it wasn't because we were mad, we just didn't know what to say. It was all so . . ."

"Awkward," Doris adds.

"Awkward is the perfect word," Jessie Rae says.

Modine shrugs, "But then nobody tells you what to do, it's not like it's written up in the 'Aunt Sally Cares' column or anything."

"That's the thing," Maggie says. "I didn't know what to do either. Then people started passing me on the street not speaking. I knew I couldn't take it if you all acted that way so I hid out."

"But we're not people, we're your friends."

"Oh, Lord, ya'll. I got so paranoid."

Jessie Rae Moore is pretty as a picture, but so timid that for years Maggie thought she was backward. Now her eyes dart everywhere. "I want you to know that leaving Steven and making your own living . . . well, I think it's wonderful . . ." Then she gasps, "Oh, my, that did sound ugly. It's not that I'm for divorce, you understand. I'm not. But the thing is . . ."

"The thing is . . ." Modine interrupts.

Jessie Rae's face is earnest. "If you were that unhappy, well, I think it's the bravest thing I ever heard of."

Maggie's eyes well. "Thanks, Jessie Rae."

"Well, you're entirely welcome. I mean, I for one have never done anything the least bit brave in my life. So I decided it was time to get started. Tommy's still fussing about that time I let you color my hair . . ."

Mrs. Mabes snorts. "Bullshit and applesauce. He wasn't fussing about the color. It didn't have a thing to do with the color. Why, everyone knows Tommy Moore is tight as Dick's hatband."

"The Lord, Mama, that was completely uncalled for!"

Mrs. Mabes's head bobs alarmingly, but her lips twitch with a satisfied smile.

Jessie Rae's face is white as powder. "Well, maybe Tommy *is* tight as Dick's hatband. But he's not the one walking around with roots down to there. So I said, 'Tommy. I'm putting my foot down. I'm making a standing appointment once a month for some of that 104 hair color even if *you* do think Maggie's on the brink of divorce and utter doom." Jessie's voice trails off in confusion, then she takes a deep breath and continues. "Sorry, Maggie. I didn't mean . . ."

Maggie's voice is faint. "That's all right, Jessie Rae."

"That was part of it too," Modine says. "You leaving Steven after all those years like to have scared all the husbands to death. We had to wait for them to settle down."

"But the thing is," Doris says, and her eyes are misty, "we've missed you. We just hope you'll forgive us for staying away so long."

Tears sting Maggie's eyes at this unexpected kindness, then suddenly she is gulping and crying. Hands reach out to her, voices murmur, "Law me, where's the Kleenex? Someone get her a glass of water."

"Oh, Lord," she stammers. "I didn't mean to cry . . . I didn't expect . . ." Then she covers her face with her hands and cries even harder.

Someone pats her shoulder. "Oh, sweetie, don't take on so."

"Come on, sugar doodle. It's gonna be all right," Shirley croons.

Maggie's lips twitch at the phrase *sugar doodle.*

Shirley's voice is choked with emotion. "Ya'll are so nice to come down here."

Some of the woman are crying, others are oohing and aahing.

"I didn't mean to fall apart," Maggie says.

Modine dabs her eyes. "I don't see anyone falling apart. Do y'all see anyone falling apart?"

Someone sniffs. "Not me."

"Me neither."

"Oh, Lord," Maggie says. "Leave it to me to have my nervous breakdown in public."

"Well, I don't know what the world's coming to if a person can't have a nervous breakdown now and then," Modine says. "I'm fixing to do that very thing as soon as I get a spare moment."

Some of the women sniff, others titter.

Jessie Rae's face is solemn. "Cry all you want, Maggie Sweet. Get it out of your system. But I do want you to write down my hair appointment, that is, if I haven't caught you at a bad time."

"Lord, Jessie Rae," Modine hoots. "If I haven't caught you at a bad time!"

Jessie Rae blushes.

Doris's eyes flash. "For goodness' sake, Modine! Why do you joke about everything. Don't take it personal, Jessie Rae. That's just how she is. Why I've actually seen Modine laugh at funerals."

Modine lowers her head. "I know. I am awful. It's just everyone's standing around saying, 'Don't he look good? Don't he look natural?' And I just want to shout, 'He looks dead, you all. Can't you see the man's dead?'"

Someone giggles nervously, then there's a gasp and a moan, and suddenly everyone is laughing. They laugh until they are holding their sides and tears are running down their faces.

"Sorry, Jessie Rae!" Modine howls. "I'm not laughing at you."

"It's just . . . we've been pent up too long," Shirley roars.

"Can't you see the man's dead! Now that *is* funny," Jessie Rae says, and her eyes are shining.

"Stop, you all! My stomach's killing me."

"Oh, mercy! My face hurts."

"Stop it! I mean it," Doris shouts.

Their faces twitch and their shoulders shake as they try to settle down. Somehow they control themselves even when Doris hiccups, but when they notice Mrs. Mabes tapping her foot and giving them her I'm-gonna-knock-the-fool-out-of-you look, they are lost again.

"We're acting like children!" Modine shrieks.

"Children fixing to get grounded."

"Oh, me, I can't stand it!"

"Oh, my, we're slap-happy."

Doris takes a deep, ragged breath. "I think we're high-sterical!"

"Doris always says high-sterical!" Modine shrieks.

"Oh, Lord, I got a stitch in my side."

"Stop, y'all. I'm about to be sick."

"I'm about to pee."

"Stop! I mean it!"

The laughter gets quieter, with longer spaces in between. Then sighing and exhausted, they settle down.

Finally, Shirley says, "See, Mama. I told you it wouldn't get ugly."

But Shirley's only answer is the sound of clanging wind chimes and a slamming door.

Shirley shrugs. "Sorry, y'all. I think Mama needs more fiber in her diet!"

They fight for control, then they're off again, five middle-aged women holding their sides, laughing until the tears come, having the nervous breakdown they've postponed for too long.

On Sunday, as Maggie drives to the cookout, she tells herself over and over again, "Take a deep breath. Don't panic. You can do this if you don't panic."

She's felt so much better since her friends had visited her at the Curl & Swirl. But she is afraid to get too relaxed. It's the first time since the class reunion that she and Jerry will be going to the same place. But even though they are going separately, there is no doubt in her mind that everyone will be watching. One false move and their secret will be out.

Why, even before the cookout they'd almost messed up. She'd told Mary Price *they'd* bring a banana pudding. It hadn't hit her until last night that only *couples* brought the same dish. If nothing was going on between them, they'd not only arrive separately, they'd take separate dishes. So she was taking the banana pudding and Jerry was taking corn chips and a red dip called salsa that he'd whipped up that morning.

"Take a deep breath. Don't panic," she repeats as she parks in front of Mary Price's house.

She glances at the cars clogging the driveway and sees that Jerry hasn't arrived. As she carries the banana pudding toward the house, she nods at the men. They are standing around a horseshoe pit, smoking, swapping fish stories, and discussing world events like the Atlanta

Braves versus all-comers and the merits of gas grills over charcoal grills.

She sighs with relief. It's a typical married-couples cookout. The women inside and the men outside, just like a junior high dance. Why, except for sitting at the same picnic tables to eat, the men and women would scarcely see each other all day.

She carries the banana pudding into the kitchen and sets it on the counter. The women are drinking coffee, organizing the food, and explaining to Jessie Rae, once again, why her congealed salad hasn't quite jelled. Then they move on to summer vacations, back-to-school shopping, and impossible husbands.

Doris is saying, "I've never thought about divorcing Knoxie. Murder. Yes. But never divorce."

Suddenly the room goes quiet and Doris say, "Oh, Lord, Maggie. I'm sorry . . . I didn't mean . . ."

Mary Price grins and puts her arm around Maggie's shoulders. "Maggie doesn't mind. She's the expert on impossible husbands, aren't you, darlin'?"

Maggie manages a lame, "I could write a book." But everyone laughs and the moment passes.

She's carrying a tray loaded with deviled eggs, slaw, and baked beans out to the picnic table, when she spots Jerry filling a washtub with ice, Coca-Cola, and beer. He smiles, throws up his hand, and calls, "Hey, Maggie. You doing all right?"

"Doing fine. Hope you are," she says, trying to keep her face friendly, but not too friendly.

A moment later, the women start carrying trays of food, paper plates, cups, and napkins outside. Then Hoyt sets platters of hamburgers and hot dogs on the table and calls, "Come on, y'all. It's ready!"

After they eat, the younger children roast marshmallows. Hoyt and Mary Price, who is dressed like Daisy Dukes in *The Dukes of Hazzard*, sing golden oldies from the sixties and seventies.

Jerry's blue eyes meet Maggie's as everyone giggles through the "ya, ya, ya, ya," chorus of "Little Darlin'."

At dusk, the children catch lightning bugs in mayonnaise jars and the adults talk about the old days versus nowadays. Typewriters compared to computers. Record player and boom boxes. Country western crossing over to rock and roll. Then the women start carrying bowls and silverware back to the kitchen. While the women are washing up, the men load the cars with coolers, soft balls, badminton nets, and children.

Forty-five minutes later everyone is backing out of the driveway and calling out good-byes.

Maggie is wiping up the kitchen counter when Jerry comes up behind her and kisses the back of her neck. She turns, smiles, and puts her arms around him.

"What do you think?" she says.

"I think I love you to pieces."

"I mean, how do you think today went?"

"It went fine, it went better than fine. And yesterday, well, you told me about what happened at the Curl & Swirl, but I wish you could have heard what Ellis and Knoxie said."

"Oh, Lord, maybe I don't want to know."

"But it was great, honey. They said if all those women descended on them they'd have run a mile. But you not only stood up for yourself, it ended peacefully and y'all are still friends. Knoxie said, 'Just goes to show I don't know a thing about women. I mean, I never thought Maggie had it in her. But when push comes to shove she can be downright feisty.'"

Maggie laughs. "Me, feisty? Oh, Lord. If they only knew how my heart was pounding."

"Yeah, but you did it."

Maggie's voice is full of wonder. "Oh, gosh. I did, didn't I?"

"Yep. And you know what else?"

"What?"

"I think you hung the moon."

28

Betty pulls into the driveway. It's been a long day at the nursing home and now she's running late. Tonight, she and Mama Dean are taking Maggie's girls to Millie's Percolator Grill for their going-off-to-school dinner.

She hurries into the house, taking the porch steps two at a time. But Mama Dean is sitting in the rocking chair by the window sprinkling herself with baby powder. She is dressed in nothing but a dingy white slip and tannish-orange panty hose that are twisted around her ankles.

Betty pulls down the shade. "Lord, Mama, why are you sitting in front of the window in your slip? And why aren't you ready? We're supposed to be taking the girls out in thirty minutes."

Mama Dean just looks at her, then stands and starts tugging her stockings up over her calves, then her knees, then her thighs. She has just started the almighty struggle of pulling them up over her white cotton bloomers when she flops back into the chair, winded.

"Law, me, I need to rest a minute."

Betty's neck feels tight. "I can't believe it! I laid out your clothes before I left for work this morning. You've had ten solid hours to get ready."

Mama Dean just glares at her. "These panty hose don't fit."

"Well, don't wear them, then. It's ninety-six degrees. You're so hot-natured anyway, you'll just burn up."

Mama Dean looks at her.

Betty sighs. "All right. I'll help you."

Mama Dean stands, then waggles her hips while Betty pulls and tugs. "Suck in your stomach, Mama," she orders, leaning into her. "Now wiggle again."

By the time the stockings are on and straightened, they are both winded and sweating.

Betty leaves the room, returning with Mama Dean's dress, shoes and hair brush. "Now get ready and hurry!"

"I can't believe you're fussing at me just because I'm a little behind schedule."

Betty's eyes go wide. *Schedule? What schedule? Was* As the World Turns *delayed? Did* General Hospital *go into overtime? Let me tell you about schedules, Mama. I've been on my feet since five this morning. I've dressed, fed, and fussed over a dozen Alzheimer patients and none of them as difficult as you!* But she doesn't say anything. She just takes a deep breath and tries to keep her voice steady. "I'm going to get dressed. When I get back, I want you to be ready. All right?"

She rushes to the bathroom, but she doesn't have time to shower. She washes, then dabs on cologne and makeup. She'd looked forward to this dinner all week. She'd even daydreamed that by tonight some miracle would happen and Maggie would be going with them. But that wasn't going to happen. Maggie was avoiding them again. Then there was Jill. Something was really bothering Jill. Oh, Lord, why were they even having this dinner with everything in such a mess? But what else could they do? Amy was leaving for school next week and they couldn't put it off any longer.

Betty glances in the mirror and smoothes her hair. She thinks about the envelopes hidden in the bottom of her purse—envelopes with crisp hundred-dollar bulls tucked inside greeting cards that urged her granddaughters to follow their dreams. She'd imagined the tender, touching moment when she gave them the cards. She'd gaze into their eyes and smile, then she'd hug them and whisper a few words of grandmotherly wisdom.

But the evening hasn't even started and she's already fresh out of smiles and hugs. Most of all she's fresh out of wisdom.

She thinks about Charlie and wishes someone would tell her to follow her dreams. He'd called last night to say he'd be in Charlotte next week. Now all she wants to do is soak in a bubble bath and think about what she'll wear, what they'll talk about, the way his eyes light up when he sees her.

She's thought about Charlie, almost nothing else, ever since the day he came into her life. But they have so many strikes against them. They live five hours apart. He's a world traveler. She's so small-town that a trip to the beach is a major event. He's retired to a good life, surrounded by friends, while work and family problems fill her days and keep her awake at night.

She's been kidding herself, daydreaming like a love-struck teenager. She has so little to offer. Why would a man like Charlie wait around for her to sort out her life when there were dozens of younger, prettier women? Jobless, childless, motherless women with nothing to do but concentrate on him?

Oh, Lord.

She doesn't feel much different than she had in her thirties, but the truth is, she isn't thirty or forty. She isn't even fifty. If she lets this chance go by in a few short years she'll be sixty, then seventy. Just another sad older woman with nothing to look forward to but duty-visits from family, the Senior Center, and Meals-on-Wheels.

She takes a deep breath and thinks about that day at Belews Pond. The day she realized how fear and shame had stunted her life.

How could she have forgotten? How could she have fallen back into her old habits? She was taking everyone's problems on herself. Losing sleep, making herself sick because a part of her still believed if she was nice enough, tried hard enough, worried long enough, she could fix everyone. Just as if that life-changing day at the pond never happened.

But Maggie had Jerry. She'd get on with her life.

Jill is seventeen, about to go off to school, with her whole life ahead of her.

Even Mama Dean, who claims to be worrying herself to death, hasn't missed a single church circle meeting much less a bingo or poker night.

Betty is the only one who's put her life on hold. Well, it's her turn. She counts, too. The last time she'd had a long talk with Charlie, he'd listened patiently, then said, "Do what you can, then let them get on with it."

Well, that's what she intends to do. She isn't about to walk away from a man who goes out of his way for her, a man she can talk to, a man whose face lights up when he sees her.

She glances at her watch, then rushes back to the living room, determined to make the best of today. But Mama Dean hasn't moved. She's still sitting there in her slip and panty hose, exactly as Betty left her.

Why, the mood Mama Dean is in, she'll probably have to sneak the girls their cards in the parking lot. Instead of the tender words she'd imagined, she'll end up whispering, "I want you to have this, but whatever you do, don't tell Mama Dean."

"Good grief, Mama. Why won't you work with me?" She pulls the dress over her mother's head, then stuffs her arms through the sleeves. Then a few quick strokes with the hairbrush and a trace of pink lipstick.

"That's enough, Betty!" Mama Dean says, twisting in her chair. "You'd think we was having supper with Johnny Cash and the Carter sisters."

"I want it to be nice. I want you to be nice."

Mama Dean juts out her jaw. "I am nice! I just don't believe in all this fuss. Why, Jill's barely said hey or kiss my foot all week. And that Amy with all her fine la-di-dah airs . . . Well, I'll not say another word. Hand me my purse and let's get this over with."

Betty feels defeated. But as she bends to pick up Mama Dean's purse from under the end table, she spots two envelopes sticking out of the top of it, envelopes with the names Jill and Amy written in Mama Dean's large, childish scrawl. She stuffs the envelopes back inside, snaps the purse shut, and imagines Mama Dean saying, "Now, girls. I want you to have this. But whatever you do, don't tell your grandy."

Betty pats Mama Dean's shoulder as she hands her the purse. "Well, Mama, look at it this way. It's my treat and everyone says the Percolator has the best steak sandwiches in town."

29

Jill

● ●

Millie's Percolator Grill is a fair-sized rectangular room with baskets of artificial ivy hanging in every window, a row of booths along one wall, and fifteen or so tables covered with blue-checkered tablecloths. In the center of each table are salt and pepper shakers, tiny baskets with packets of sugar and Equal, and a cobalt-blue Milk of Magnesia bottle filled with pink and mauve zinnias.

While they wait to be seated, Jill sighs and drums her fingers on the counter. But as they're led to a table in the back she reminds herself to behave.

They are getting settled when the waitress, Angie Blevins, who graduated last year but already has a baby, fills their water glasses and tells them about the day's specials.

Jill nods, pretending to take it all in, but she's just going through the motions and a moment later she drifts off again. She's been hiding out in her room all week, ever since she saw her father and Mrs. Bloodworth at the flea market. If she had her way, she'd still be hiding out, but Grandy and Mama Dean wouldn't leave her alone.

They kept checking on her, Grandy tapping on her door, saying, "Are you all right, sugar? Do you want to talk? Why don't you have a bite to eat with us?"

Grandy seemed to think that life was a Norman Rockwell painting—that if they ate meals from the four basic food groups and talked things through, everything would be all right. But Grandy didn't know what was really going on. Sometimes Jill wondered how someone that old could be so innocent. Why, Jill was barely out of high school and she already knew the world was crap.

But it was Mama Dean who was really driving her crazy. She'd barge into Jill's room without knocking. Then she's stand there with her hands on her hips saying things like, "Jill Kayroley Presson, what in the Sam Hill are you doing?"

Sometimes she'd come out of her room long enough to straighten the house or start supper or wash a few dishes. But she only did it so Mama Dean would leave her in peace. Other times she just covered her head with a pillow until Mama Dean went away. But by today she'd wanted to shout, "Who the hell is Sam Hill anyway? And don't call me Jill Kayroley! I've spent my whole life telling you it's not Kayroley, it's Jill Carole! Carol with an *e* on the end of it. I'm seventeen years old! Don't you think it's time my own great-grandmother knew how to pronounce my name? But no matter what she said Mama Dean never got it right. Of course she also called shrivel "swivel," author "Arthur," and girls named Sara "Sayree."

This morning, Jill had finally left the house. Not because she had anyplace to go, but because she was afraid she'd lose it completely and yell at Mama Dean. She'd spent the day wandering aimlessly through town, lost in her own thoughts. Once, she'd stopped for coffee, but she had so much on her mind she'd just sat and stared until the coffee got cold and it was time to move on. But no matter what she did all she could think about was her father. She thought about the years her mother walked the floors over suppers that had dried out in the oven while they waited for him to come home from one of his oh-so-important meetings. But what if all those years he'd really been messing around with Mrs. Bloodworth? And Mama. Poor Mama. Everyone blamed her for breaking up the family. She and Amy had been so mean about it they'd made their mother cry. What if Mama left home because she found out about Daddy and Mrs. Bloodworth?

Jill jerks herself back to reality. Amy is sitting across from her, fanning herself with her menu while she goes on and on about what she'll wear the first day at Chapel Hill, the sorority she'll pledge, and how scholarships like hers were given to only a few of the most amazingly brilliant.

Jill ignores her and drifts off again, but she's slammed back to earth when Amy says, "Daddy took me to the mall and bought me a whole new wardrobe. He said nothing but Belk's would do."

Jill's neck feels hot. She'd planned to be good. She owed that much to Grandy and Mama Dean, who were trying to make tonight special. But Amy had pushed and pushed until it was all she could do not to stand up and shout, "Daddy! Daddy! Let me tell you about your precious Daddy." But she doesn't say anything. She just looks at her sister and mouths the words, "Shut the hell up, Amy."

But Amy smirks at her, looks her straight in the eye, and says, "I know I'm going on and on, but I'm so excited. I mean, in just one week, I'll be surrounded by intelligent people."

That's when Jill reaches under the table and pinches her, hard, on the leg.

Amy makes a sound like a startled blue jay.

Grandy and Mama Dean, who have been studying their menus look up, confused, but before they can take in what's happened, Angie is back, licking her pencil, tucking her hair behind her ears and saying, "Are you all ready to order?"

Jill stares at Amy, daring her to say something, but when Amy lowers her eyes, Jill knows it's over. Amy would rather die than risk a scene in public.

They place their orders—steak sandwiches, Texas fries, and iced tea all around, followed by lemon ice-box pie.

After Angie goes back to the kitchen, Grandy and Mama Dean lean forward. Their seats creak and rustle as they slide envelopes across the table. Jill stares at hers, confused. But Amy rips hers open and her voice is high with excitement as she leaps from her chair and circles the table to hug both grandmothers.

Jill sits there in a fog until she realizes everyone is staring at her and Grandy is saying, "Jill, honey, aren't you going to open yours?"

She nods, but her hands are clumsy as she picks up the envelope and opens it slowly. Grandy's card says, "At last your hopes are about to come true. You are on your way to great things. Congratulations, Granddaughter." She opens the card, closes it quickly, then opens it again. She can't believe it! Grandy has given her a hundred-dollar bill.

Now, Mama Dean is saying, "Come on, Miss-Slow-as-Molasses, open mine too."

Mama Dean's card is covered with dancing bunnies dressed in gingham bonnets and dotted-swiss pinafores. It says, "To a sweet little granddaughter. Hallelujah and hippety-hoppety-hooray!" Inside the card is a check for twenty dollars.

"It's for school!" Grandy says. "It's for whatever you need for school. We're so proud of you, sugar."

Jill sits there, trying to figure out what to do. How can she tell them she's not going to school, that after next week she doesn't even know where she'll be staying.

Now, Grandy is reaching over and patting her hand. "Oh, Jill, honey. We didn't mean to make you cry."

Jill is silent all the way home. When they pull into her father's driveway, Amy gets out of the car, goes around to the driver's seat to hug Grandy, then to Mama Dean in the passenger's seat. Jill is so busy staring up at the house that it catches her off-guard when Amy opens her door, gives her a quick awkward hug, and says, "Hey, Jill. I'll see you."

"Yeah, Aim, see ya," she mumbles. She tries not to feel anything as her twin slams the car door and walks toward the house.

The minute they get back to Grandy's, she goes straight to her room. She lies on her bed, listening, as Mama Dean says good night, then closes her bedroom door. She hears Grandy moving around in the kitchen: filling the coffeepot, setting boxes of cereal and bowls on the counter, then a loaf of bread, jars of honey and jam near the toaster for morning.

It isn't until she hears Grandy's door sigh shut that she gets out of bed and goes up the hall and knocks.

"Grandy," she says, as the door opens. "I know I'm a jerk. But I need to talk to you."

30

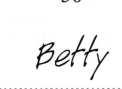

Betty prides herself on never losing her temper, but as she drives home at midnight, after working second shift, she can't get last night's scene with Jill out of her mind. The child was trembling when she'd knocked on the door.

"I lied, Grandy," she said, ducking her head, avoiding Betty's eyes. "I'm not going off to school. I just told you that because I didn't know what else to do."

"But Jill . . . you said . . . your daddy said . . ."

"I know. But he just said it . . . he never really meant it . . . Oh, Grandy, we had a fight. I took off." Jill's face seemed to crumble. "It was awful."

Betty didn't know what to do or say. But when she heard her granddaughter's deep, ragged breath, she put her arms around her and held her tight.

"I'm sorry I lied, Grandy. I'm sorry to be so much trouble. As soon as I get a job, I promise I'll move out."

Betty had never felt so sorry for anyone in all her life. "Oh, sweetie, " she'd said. "You're not a bit of trouble. You can stay with me as long as you like."

After Jill settled down and went back to bed, Betty spent the rest of the night tossing and turning. It is all she could do not to get out of bed, drive over to Steven's, and shake him, hard. How can he be so cold, so hateful? It was bad enough he'd broken his promise, but Jill had left home weeks ago. In all that time Steven hasn't so much as called to speak to his daughter. No wonder the girl was miserable. No wonder she feels like a burden when her own father doesn't seem to care. "He has to have everything approved by him. *Everything!* It's always been my way or the highway with Steven." That's what Maggie had said.

And Maggie? Does Maggie know Steven reneged on his promise, but hasn't bothered to say anything? This flies all over Betty. Jill is staying with her. She deserves to know what's going on. How can she help if no one tells her anything? No wonder Jill has brooded around the house all week. Why, the poor child must have felt like crawling under the table at their going-away dinner last night when she knew she wasn't going anywhere. Betty sighs. Here she was innocently thinking she was doing something nice when all she was doing was making Jill feel worse.

Betty drives down East Main, past the library, the Zippy Mart, then the Curl & Swirl. Maggie's apartment is dark. It's all she can do not to knock on the door, wake Maggie up, and tell her a thing or two. Maybe there wasn't a thing Maggie could do about Steven, but it was time for her to get over herself, to stop hiding out, to have enough gumption to face everyone and be there for the girls. But that wasn't fair. Maggie had tried to see the girls and it'd been a disaster. She'd surprised Mama Dean with an Impossible Pie and it had gone completely wrong. Oh,

Lord! How could Betty have been stupid enough, desperate enough, to suggest such a thing? She should have known Mama Dean would feel ambushed and go all to pieces. Maggie had been so deep-down hurt, she'd probably never come back.

Betty has so much on her mind she doesn't realize she's missed her turn until she's on the second block of West Main. She's slowing the car, looking for a place to turn around, when she spots him. It's Steven! He's coming out of Theo Bloodworth's house. Betty shakes her head to clear it. How odd, to see him, just when she's thinking about him. She has a good mind to stop the car and have it out with him. Even if it's midnight. Even if it's old-money West Main.

Steven is smiling as he walks down the driveway toward his car. When he turns toward the house and waves, Betty notices that Theo is standing in the doorway. But it isn't until Theo leans out to return his wave and is backlit by the lights inside the foyer, that Betty sees . . . Oh, Lord . . . It can't be . . . Theo Bloodworth is wearing nothing but a pale, shimmering nightgown.

Steven and Theo! Theo and Steven! Betty thinks she must have said the words out loud, because that's when Steven whirls around, looks right at her, and raises his arms in surrender.

Saturday afternoon, Betty is stacking the lunch trays on the food cart when Angie Stutts appears, grinning. "Phone call, Betty," she whispers. "It's a man!"

Betty's eyes go wide. "A man with an English accent?"

Angie laughs. "Whoa! So you've been holding out for Paul McCartney all these years. Well, sorry to burst your bubble, but it's just some guy with a plain old American accent."

Betty wonders who in the world as she goes to the break room and picks up the phone.

"Betty, is that you?"

She takes a deep breath. It's Steven. The last person on earth she expected.

"This is awkward, but I had to call. I . . . uh . . . I want you to know that . . . about last night . . . Theo and I never . . . at least not until Maggie and I . . ."

Oh, Lord. She thinks about Steven and Theo, then Maggie and Jerry, and suddenly she's completely worn out.

Now Steven is saying, "I've always thought so highly of you, Betty. You know that. I just don't want you to think . . . well, we go back a long way . . . so you've got know I've always tried to do the right thing."

Betty wants to say, Is lying to your daughter the right thing? Is sleeping with Theo, then being holier-than-thou with Maggie the right thing? And she wants to say it at the top of her lungs.

Then it hits her. Steven is already worried. If she plays her cards right, she'll be in the catbird seat. What was it they said about southern women? Butter not melting? Catching flies with honey? Betty had never thought of herself as the charming kind, but after spending most of her fifty-six years soothing the most demanding person on the face of the earth, she was probably an expert. Why, compared to Mama Dean, when it came to difficult, Steven was barely a flyweight.

"I always said you were a good man, Steven. You and Maggie both tried for years. But sometimes people just aren't suited to each other. If you and Maggie can't work things out, I won't hold it against you."

"Ah, thanks, Betty. I hoped you'd understand."

"I understand all right. When it's over it's over. Sometimes all you can do is sign the papers and move on."

"Oh, I'm not ready for tha—"

Betty sees she's jumped in too fast. She's got to pour on more charm and pour it on thick. She presses on, talking right over him. "Like I said, you are a good man. I mean, look at your daughters. Everyone knows it takes a very special man to raise such wonderful daughters."

"I appreciate you saying—"

"Well, they are my granddaughters, so I'm bound to be partial. But Amy off to Chapel Hill with a scholarship, then Jill being accepted by Chief Too-Tall. Who would have thought? Wasn't it your friend, Theo, who said the chief was a master carver, that Jill had to be a genius to be accepted at her age?"

Steven's voice is low. "Was it? I don't remember."

"Well, I'll never forget it. She said it at the girls' graduation party. Then you said you'd pay Jill's tuition. Why, half the town was standing there in your dining room when you made the announcement. We were all so proud. I cannot tell you how much it meant to me. I don't know Theo all that well, but I've thought about calling her, you know, to thank her for encouraging Jill."

"Uh . . . I don't think that's a good idea . . ."

"Well, whatever you say, Steven. But I'm so happy for Jill. And you must be proud as a peacock."

"I am, it's just—"

"You're way too modest. Jill *is* loaded with talent. But everyone knows if it wasn't for you being so supportive, not to mention paying the tuition, why, none of this would be possible."

Steven is silent.

"Are you still there, Steven?"

"Still here," he says, sounding glazed over.

"There are just a couple of little picky things we need to talk about before we hang up. Jill seems to think that you're mad at her. Poor thing. She's so sensitive. I guess that's what they mean by artistic temperament. But why don't you give her a call now and then so she'll know everything's all right. Oh, and Steven, I know you're busy and it's probably just slipped your mind, but the tuition for Chief Too-Tall is due this week."

Steven is silent for so long Betty wonders if she's gone too far. Finally he says, "Whatever you say, Betty . . . but . . . uh . . . about last night?"

"I think we understand each other now, don't you, Steven?"

His voice is flat. "I think we understand each other perfectly."

"Of course most of the people in town probably wouldn't understand, you know, about last night and all. Maggie wouldn't. And Mama Dean . . . well, I shudder to think what Mama Dean would do if she got wind of it. But since we understand each other so well, I think we'll keep last night our little secret."

When Betty hangs up the phone all she wants to do is tap dance up the halls, turn a few cartwheels, then high-five the patients, visitors, and staff, including her supervisor, Mrs. Fayette Chupp. She doesn't do any of these things, but she can't seem to stop smiling and she catches herself humming, "I Am Woman, Hear Me Roar."

She feels as if she's someone to reckon with, like Scarlett O'Hara.

Sunday morning she wakes filled with righteous indignation. She starts the coffee, muttering, "Take that, Mr. Stuck-on-Himself Presson." Then, "How do you like that, Mr. My-Way-or-the-Highway?" as she runs the shower. At church, the only passage she hears is, "And the meek shall inherit the earth," and she whispers, "Amen."

But by Sunday afternoon, when he still hasn't called, she starts to worry. What if she went too far? Made matters worse? Got Steven's back up? What if he takes it out on Jill by refusing to pay her tuition or never, in this lifetime, speaking to her again?

And Maggie. What if, out of spite, he never signs the divorce papers? Or drags it out forever? Or drags it out long enough to find out about Maggie and Jerry?

Oh, Lord.

She goes to the kitchen to start supper. Last Sunday they'd had pot roast, potatoes, and baby carrots cooked in Lipton's Onion Soup Mix, which meant tonight is fried chicken, mashed potatoes, and snap-bean night. They'd had the same every other weekend menu for years, but today it seems as complicated as Thanksgiving with all the trimmings. She breads the chicken, then scrubs the potatoes, and pops everything in the oven. Tonight it would be baked chicken and potatoes or a visit to the hospital's quiet room. But, even this isn't simple enough. Thirty minutes later, she wanders out to the kitchen and sees she's forgotten to turn on the oven.

She double-checks the oven, sets the timer, and double-checks it, too. Then she goes out to the garden to pick tomatoes for a salad.

She'd thought she was so clever when she'd made Steven stammer. She'd felt downright smug when he fell for her honeyed words. But she should have known better. Every time she'd even considered being smug, God or something came along to thump her on the head and mash her down to size.

She might have been born in the South, but when it came to playing a Steel Magnolia she'd always be a tourist.

Now, why was wandering around in the yard, anyway? Oh, yeah, tomatoes for salad.

She's back inside washing the lettuce when the telephone rings. She rinses her hands and is reaching for a dish towel when Jill comes out of her room and grabs the phone on the third ring.

Betty goes back to the salad, until she hears her granddaughter say, "Daddy!"

Betty holds her breath and turns off the water, but Jill stretches the phone cord around the corner into the half bath.

Betty's whole body strains toward the closed door, but Jill's voice is too low to make out any words. She has an impulse to tiptoe across the kitchen and press her ear against the door, but she wills herself to toss the salad and wait, even though her heart is pounding.

A few minutes later Jill comes out of the bathroom, hangs up the phone, and starts back toward her room.

Betty thinks she might run down the street screaming if the suspense lasts much longer. "Jill, is everything all right?"

Jill turns and her face is pale. "That was Daddy. He says he's going to pay my tuition after all."

"That's wonderful. But, for goodness' sakes, sugar, you don't look very happy."

"I don't know. It's just . . ." Jill looks at Betty, then looks away.

"Just what?"

"It's just . . . just when I decide he's a jerk, that he'll probably be a jerk forever he calls. Now I'm all mixed up."

"I know you're upset, but it's not right to talk about your daddy that way."

"I know, it's just . . . things have been so bad for so long, you know, between Daddy and me . . . then Mama and Daddy . . . Oh, Grandy, it's like I don't believe anything anymore."

Betty dries her hands. "Sit down. I'll fix us some tea. We need to talk." She pours two glasses and carries them to the table. "I know it's a mess and I hate that you've having such a hard time. But your mother and daddy love you."

Jill frowns into her glass. "Well, they sure have a weird way of showing it."

"I know. But they're only human, just two flawed human beings."

Jill snorts. "You've got that right."

Betty sighs. "I know they've made lots of mistakes. But now they're trying to do different. Don't you see, Jill? Sometimes all you can do, when you make a mistake, is to go back and try to do different."

"But how can I trust . . . what if he changes his mind again?"

"He won't."

Jill sits up straighter, then slumps and her eyes go flat. "Come on, Grandy. How can you know such a thing?"

Betty closes her eyes and thinks of her bargain with Steven. Leave it to Jill to ask the one question she can never answer. She leans forward and smiles playfully. "All I can say is, I know what I know."

Jill's chin quivers. "Don't tease, Grandy. It's too important."

Betty reaches across the table and pats her granddaughter's arm. "Oh, sugar, I don't know how to explain it. But, all right, here goes. Do you remember when you were little? You and Amy thought I could see around corners and through walls."

Jill nods, remembering. "Yeah. Mama told us you had eyes in the back of your head. We believed it, too. I still can't figure out how you always knew what we were up to."

"Oh, Jill, I don't know what everyone's up to or how other things will work out with your daddy. But when it comes to your classes with the chief . . . let's just call it intuition."

On Tuesday, Betty is sliding a tray through the cafeteria line at work when Maggie comes up behind her. "Oh, Mother, you'll never believe what's happened."

A moment before the cafeteria had been filled with the sounds of banging trays, clanging silverware, voices and laughter, but suddenly the room goes silent as everyone strains forward hoping to catch the latest installment of the Sweet family saga.

Betty gives a warning look, but keeps her voice light as if Maggie turns up for lunch every day. "I'm glad you could make it. Get a tray. Let's see . . . the spaghetti looks kinda dry today, but the chicken and dumplings look good."

They fill their plates and keep their faces blank as they carry their trays outside to the farthest patio table.

"Tell me quick," Betty says, glancing all around. "It's been so hot, not a soul's eaten out here all summer, but now that they've seen you they'll be here in a heartbeat."

Maggie leans forward. "You'll never guess. Steven called. He wants my lawyer to call his lawyer. He's ready to sign the divorce papers. That means that Jerry and me . . . well, you know." She looks around. A few people are already drifting out onto the patio. She lowers her voice. "You'll never believe what else he said. He said, I think it's in the girls' best interest if we try to act civilized."

"Oh, Maggie!"

Maggie's eyes sparkle and she seems to be sitting up straighter in her chair. "Of course, I said that weeks ago, but before I could remind him, he said he'd talked to Amy. Oh, Mother, she actually got on the phone and *we* talked! It was a little awkward, you know, overpolite and all, but at least we talked."

"Oh, sugar, that's wonderful and I told you he'd called Jill about paying her tuition."

Maggie nods. "I know. I still can't hardly believe it."

"Course that means she'll be staying here in town so that'll give y'all a chance to . . . well, you know."

Maggie smiles, then looks depressed again. "I know. I just wish Amy'd be around for a while. She's leaving for Chapel Hill on Sunday."

Betty looks at Maggie, then looks away. "I know," she says quietly. "Jill and I . . . we're going over to the house to see her off."

Maggie's face is pale. "Oh, gosh. I never thought about that."

Betty pats her hand. "Well, it's not like we're going to get to spend any real time with her. There'll be a bunch of people kind of standing around the driveway, her friends from school, a couple of neighbors . . ."

Tears spring to Maggie's eyes and she lowers her head.

"Oh, honey, I hate you can't be there."

Maggie pushes the chicken and dumplings around on her plate. "I hate it, too. Lord, Mother. Why does it always have to be one step forward and two steps back?"

"I know you're disappointed, but Amy *did* call, Jill's taking those classes with the chief, and Steven's wanting to be civilized. Why, a few days ago we didn't think that would ever happen. That's more like three or four steps forward and only one back."

"You're right. I need to look on the bright side, but it's hard when it comes to the girls."

For a while neither of them says anything. Maggie looks around the room and nods at a couple of people, then says, "Honestly, Mother, what do you think's come over Steven?"

Betty swirls the ice in her glass searching for something to say. "I don't know. He's getting older, you know. Maybe he's done some soul-searching these last few weeks."

"Yeah, right," Maggie says, but a moment later her eyes go wide. "Unless . . . good Lord, Mother, do you think he's seeing Theo Bloodworth?"

Betty gasps. "Well, Maggie . . ."

"It *is* possible!"

"Well, for goodness' sake."

Maggie stares off into the distance, deep in thought. "They've been going to the same tombstone rubbings for years and they're on the same wavelength, both of them being such snobs and all. But Theo's into art. She thinks Jill's some kind of artistic genius and all of a sudden Steven's willing to forget computer school and pay for carving classes?"

Betty sighs. It's on the tip of her tongue to say, I don't know. But the truth is she does know and even though she can't say what she's thinking, she can't flat out lie.

"Lord, Maggie. I swear I don't know what to think anymore. But say, for instance, it was true about . . . you know . . . about them . . . would it . . . uh . . . bother you?"

"I hadn't really thought about it . . . but, no . . . I don't think so. Used to, I'd get so aggravated the way he compared me with Miss Historical-Society-President. But Theo's all right in her way."

Betty holds her breath, wondering how to get off the subject of Steven and Theo. She doesn't exhale until Maggie takes a bite of her lunch and says, "You're right, Mother. The chicken and dumplings are good."

Neither of them says anything for a while. Finally, Maggie says, "What time are you going to see Amy off?"

"Around noon, I guess. Why?"

Maggie sighs. "I bought her some things. A sweater set, a backpack, some stationery, you know. Would you mind taking them for me?"

"Sure, sweetie, I'll be glad to."

Maggie pushes her plate away.

"Aren't you going to finish?"

Maggie slumps in her seat. "I lost my appetite."

"Are you all right?"

"Yeah. I'm all right. But, I'll tell you what! Theo Bloodworth better not be there on Sunday."

"But I thought you said you wouldn't mind."

Maggie's eyes flash. "I don't care what Steven and Theo get up to, but hotalmightydamn, Mother! She better not be seeing Amy off if I can't!"

That night, after supper, instead of washing dishes right away, as usual, Betty follows Mama Dean to the front room. Mama Dean sinks into her rocking chair by the window and picks up the remote, but before she can click the TV on, Betty says, "Wait a minute, Mama. We need to talk."

Mama Dean clicks on the TV anyway, but keeps the sound low. It's a rerun of *Knots Landing*.

Betty sits on the couch as close to her mother as possible. "I saw Maggie today."

Mama Dean turns up the volume. Karen is comforting Val, who's crying about something Gary's done.

When Mama Dean sets the remote on the end table, Betty picks it up, flicks it off, and stuffs it under a couch cushion. "I know you don't want to talk about this, but I'm too old to be sneaking around to see my own daughter. Steven is signing the divorce papers."

Mama Dean sighs, "Law, me . . . "

"She'll be all right. She has a job . . . that apartment behind the shop . . ."

Mama Dean raises her hand in a warning. "Stop. I'm too old for all this."

"I know you're upset. We've all been upset. But they're about to go through with it, like it or not."

"Well, I don't. I don't like it nary a bit. I tell you they'll be weeping and wailing and . . . " Mama Dean crosses her arms over her chest and starts rocking.

"Lord, Mama. No one likes it. But it's a cold hard fact. We need to try to keep it friendly for the girls' sake."

Mama Dean snorts. "Friendly!"

"I know it won't be easy, but it wasn't right the way we did it. I spent my whole life feeling sorry as gully dirt about my divorce. But at least I had Maggie. Maggie has to park out front just to sneak a glimpse of her girls. Why, she's not even welcomed here in the house she was raised in."

"Don't ask me to see her. I'm not ready." Mama Dean folds her hands in her lap and stares at them.

"Well, you need to get ready."

Mama Dean gnaws her bottom lip.

Betty's voice is hushed, barely a whisper. "Oh, Mama. You've got a right to be upset. You've got a right to be mad. But this has gone on too long. Are you planning to stay mad your whole life?"

Mama Dean glares at her. "You don't know how I feel."

"I know enough. I know you sitting here all sulled up isn't helping anyone, not even you. I know *we're* about to fall out over this."

Mama Dean ducks her head.

Betty leans forward. "Maggie's been your granddaughter all her life and she's been good to you. She's hurting too, Mama. Hurting as much as you. Maybe more."

Mama Dean meets Betty's eyes, then looks away.

"Lord, Mama, can't you see? If you don't get past this, you're going to lose her. I don't want that to happen."

Neither of them says anything for a while. Finally Betty says, "I nearly forgot. Amy's leaving for school on Sunday. Jill and I are going over there to see her off. You'll have to get someone to carry you to church or, better yet, you could come with us."

Mama Dean stares at her hands folded in her lap.

Betty sighs, sets the remote back on the end table and stands. As she heads toward the kitchen to clear supper dishes, she hears the TV click on and her eyes well with defeat. It's all she can do not to shout, "I'm through, Mama. I'm through being in the middle. I'm through defending Maggie to you, explaining you to her. I won't live in a place where my own daughter isn't welcomed."

31

Betty

....

Saturday night Betty sleeps soundly, then wakes with a jolt around three. That's when it hits her. Today, when she goes to see Amy, will be the first time she's been to the old house on Morehead since Maggie left Steven last spring. And Steven. She hadn't seen him for months, right up until that night she'd caught him sneaking out of Theo Bloodworth's and all but blackmailed him. Oh, Lord. How can she face him and pretend everything is all right?

Stop, she reminds herself. She hasn't done a thing to feel guilty about. It's just a pity she had to resort to blackmail to get him to do the right thing.

But as hard as it would be for her it would be even harder for Jill. Jill hadn't laid eyes on her daddy or been back to her own house for weeks. Now her twin was leaving, and even though they didn't always get along, it was bound to feel like some kind of ending. Oh, my. She'd have to remember to keep an eye on Jill.

By now Betty is wide awake and worried about everything: Maggie. Mama Dean. Would Theo be there today? What about

Steven's uppity mother? For nineteen years Mrs. Presson had looked down her long narrow nose at all of them. Even Maggie. Especially Maggie. Betty had watched Maggie fetch and carry and kowtow, only to be treated like some backward redneck hick. Betty had stopped going over there when Mrs. Presson visited, because all she could do was stand by helplessly while she longed to jerk a knot in the old biddy's tail.

She turns her pillow over looking for a cool, dry spot, but there aren't any. It's August, the true dog days of the longest, hottest summer she can remember.

Finally, somewhere around four, Charlie floats into her mind. Charlie, the only smooth place in her life. He'd be here on Monday. She'd see him right after work. All she has to do is get through today and everything will be all right. Then she relaxes and drifts off again until nearly seven.

While Jill dresses, Betty tidies the kitchen, loads the dishwasher, then goes into her room to change.

It's only eleven o'clock but the thermostat outside the kitchen window already registers ninety-five.

Betty sighs. She's been jumpy as a cricket ever since Mama Dean went off with Ada Jennings right after breakfast. Mama Dean hadn't said the first word about where she was going or when she'd be back. Why she hadn't so much as said "hey" or "kiss my foot." Mama Dean wasn't speaking at all.

But as she and Jill round the corner onto Morehead Street, she decides it's for the best. Even without Mama Dean she has more than she can say grace over.

When they pull into the driveway, Jill gives her a quick trembly smile, then they both get out of the car.

Steven, who is trying to force a huge suitcase into the trunk, nods in their direction. "Hey, Jill . . . Betty," he says. Then he wipes his forehead with the back of his arm and returns to struggling with the suitcase.

A moment later, Amy comes down the back porch steps with a garment bag in one hand and a cosmetic case in the other. She rushes toward them, laughing and talking a mile a minute. "Hey, y'all!"

Betty gives her a hug. "Hey, sugar. Today's the big day."

Amy nods. "I know. But Daddy's in a mood. He's been fussing at me all morning about taking too much stuff, but I swear every bit of it is ab-so-lute-ly vital."

Then she crosses the yard, shoves the case and bag in her father's direction, and walks away.

Betty decides that's one of the biggest differences between her granddaughters. Amy has always been unfazed by Steven's moods, while Jill is so tender-hearted, a raised eyebrow can wound her to the quick.

"Ya'll want some tea?" Amy asks, and they follow her into the kitchen. Betty glances around the room. It's tidy, but Maggie's baskets and mugs and prized yellow canisters are missing. Only the essentials are left, lined up with the precision of an operating room. Betty wonders if Maggie took them with her or if Steven got rid of them.

Betty whacks the ice tray so hard against the counter that the cubes go flying across the room. The girls jump and look at her and she pretends to be concentrating on setting out glasses, pouring tea and slicing a lemon. She reminds herself to count her blessings. At least Theo and Mrs. Presson aren't here and Steven's behaving himself.

She hands Amy a glass. "Carry this to your daddy. He's working hard and it's hot out there."

A few minutes later, she, Amy and Jill are sitting on the porch steps sipping their tea and talking when a big yellow car with tail fins pulls into the driveway.

Betty holds her breath as Ada Jennings gets out, followed a few seconds later by a tight-faced Mama Dean.

Ada heads toward Betty and the girls, talking the whole time. "I'm so glad we caught y'all before Amy left. Why, your Mama Dean would've felt awful if she'd missed you. I guess she didn't want to burden me by asking me to stop off on our way from church. But, when I saw y'all's car I said, well, for goodness' sake, Deanie, why didn't you tell me? You know, I love those girls like they was my own."

Mama Dean's face is pale. She works her jaw and avoids everyone's eyes.

Amy, as oblivious to Mama Dean's mood as she is to her father's, gives her a hug. "Hey, Mama Dean, Miz Jennings. I'm glad y'all stopped. This is the best day of my life."

When Amy lets go of Mama Dean to hug Ada, Mama Dean's chin quivers and there are tears in her eyes.

Betty touches her mother's arm and guides the older women to the glider in the shade of a huge magnolia tree: Maggie's old favorite thinking-things-over spot.

Mr. and Mrs. Franklin, from next door, drift into the yard, still dressed in their church clothes. They hand Amy a going-away gift, a pair of Praying Hands bookends. Amy minds her manners and thanks them politely, while Jill turns away to cover her smirk with her hands.

Mrs. Franklin joins the women on the glider and asks Mama Dean if she ever remembers a summer this hot, and what does she think about Letty Blankinship winning twenty-five dollars at bingo last week when everyone knows the bingo caller's a second cousin of Letty's.

Mr. Franklin wanders over to the driveway where Steven is moving boxes from the trunk to the seat and then back again. A few minutes later Mr. Franklin shrugs and returns to the glider to remind his wife that it's lunchtime.

Mrs. Franklin rises, takes Amy's hand, and says, confidentially, "Jesus is everywhere, even in Chapel Hill. Just remember that, Amy, and you won't go wrong."

Mr. Franklin looks skyward and says, "Amen." Then they take the shortcut between the hedges toward home.

Betty, Mama Dean, and Ada are sitting in the glider sipping iced tea. Betty stares up at the old house, remembering quiet Sunday dinners, birthdays, and Christmases, the girls at six, wearing pastel dresses and sweet, solemn faces for their first day of kindergarten. Then middle school and high school. Graduation day. She's only half listening as the two older women fan themselves with church bulletins and discuss bingo and Letty Blankinship. Ada's in favor of "letting sleeping dogs lie." Mama Dean fans harder. "For goodness' sakes, Ada! All them Blankinships is crooked as a barrel of fish hooks. Why, they need to put 'em all *under* the jail."

Amy whispers something to Jill. They both grin and disappear into the house. A few minutes later, they emerge with more boxes. Jill looks around nervously, then carries a stack to Betty's car and puts them in the backseat.

Amy boldly sets her boxes between Steven and his car, but before he can react, three of Amy's friends appear carrying Bon Voyage balloons. They're all leaving for separate schools later today. They exchange addresses, then hold hands and form a circle, and Betsy Jo Pinckney, Dr. Pinckney's daughter, leads them in a solemn chorus of Poplar Grove's high school anthem. Then, before the women in the glider can take it all in, the girls bounce up the driveway, climb into Betsy Jo's red Karman Ghia, and a moment later they are gone.

Mama Dean blinks and shakes her head, "Law, me, them girls make me swimmy-headed. They're like farts in a whirlwind."

For a while, Amy stands in the driveway staring after her friends. Betty has just decided to go over and check on her when the girl wipes her eyes and heads back to the glider. Betty hands her a Kleenex and she blows her nose then sits cross-legged on the grass near Jill.

A few minutes later, Steven honks the horn to signal that it's time to leave. The women all rise, but stand there reminding Amy to write home every week, study but have a good time, and to eat plenty of greens.

Steven waits in the car, staring straight ahead, his face unreadable. Then his eyes meet Betty's and he shakes himself and rests his head on the steering wheel.

It isn't until he honks the horn again that they start walking slowly toward the car.

They are standing in a clump near the driveway when a tan Honda pulls up.

Every jaw drops. It's Maggie.

She gets out of her car and she's crying and walking toward the girls with her arms opened wide. The girls hesitate for an instant, then they're rushing toward her, hugging and crying, their voices shrill one moment and soft as a lullaby the next. "I'm sorry. It's been awful . . . I'm so glad . . . I've missed you."

Betty thinks her heart just might stop, then Mama Dean gasps and leans into her.

Ada, unaware of what's happening, rushes toward Maggie and the girls, shouting, "Hey, Maggie Sweet. Looks like your chicks are about to fly the coop." But Maggie and the girls don't even look up and Ada's voice trails off in confusion.

Betty exhales sharply and squeezes her mother's shoulder. "Come on, Mama," she says and they take off toward the driveway. They are almost there, when Mama Dean stops suddenly, stands stock still, and wails. "I can't, Betty. Don't make me . . ."

But it's too late for that because Maggie, who must have seen them coming, is flinging her arms around them, crying, "Mother? Mama Dean? Oh, Mama Dean." An instant later the girls are beside them and everyone is weeping and talking and holding each other so closely Betty can't tell where one of them ends and the other begins.

A moment later, Ada, who's been standing on the sidelines, taps Betty on the shoulder and hands her a packet of blue tissues. When they notice she's dabbing her own eyes they pull her into the family circle.

"Oh, Ada, bless your heart," Betty says. "We love you too, don't we, y'all?"

"I swanee," Ada says, brokenly. "I've never seen a family take on so over a going-away."

Betty, Maggie, Amy, and Jill just nod and sniffle.

But Mama Dean has an answer. "Well, Lordhavemercy, Ada, that's 'cause our family's closer than most."

. . .

After Steven and Amy leave, Betty heads for home, followed by Ada with Mama Dean and Maggie with Jill.

Betty and Maggie pull their cars into the driveway, but Ada parks out front, walks Mama Dean to the door, and says, "Law me, I'm completely give out. I'm going home to take a nap, but I'll pick you up at three for the ice cream social, Deanie."

The family gathers around the kitchen table. But after their emotional morning they're all uneasy and tongue-tied, as if they have nothing to say or too many things they're not ready to say.

Betty sets out pickles, grain bread, and tuna salad, and reminds herself that even though it's awkward, they've made a real start.

After lunch, Maggie and Jill disappear outside and Mama Dean, who looks blurry-eyed, goes to her room for a nap.

Betty is straightening the kitchen when Maggie comes back inside, looks around the room, and says, "Where's Mama Dean?"

"Taking a nap."

Maggie sits at the table. "Good. She looked completely worn out."

"I know, I'm exhausted, but it's worth it. The whole day's been like an answer to a prayer."

Maggie's eyes well up and she reaches into her purse for a tissue. "Oh, Mother, when Jill and I were outside she showed me her workshop. I was hoping she took me there so we could have a heart-to-heart talk, but then it hit me. Jill showing me her workshop *is* a heart-to-heart talk."

Betty pats her daughter's hand and neither of them says anything for a while.

Finally, Betty says, "I thought it'd break my heart to see your old house again, and it was hard, but it was so sweet to see your girls talking and laughing together after all this time."

Maggie's face is wistful.

Betty smiles. "Did you notice even Steven behaved himself."

"Lord, Mother, he was scared to death. All us women crying and carrying on and in public."

Betty laughs. "What did you think when Mama Dean said our family is closer than most."

"She was showing out for Miz Jennings."

"I know. But thanks to Miz Jennings even Mama Dean behaved. Now I'm going to clean up from lunch while you call a certain someone."

"Call him from here?"

"You've got to let him know what happened. He's probably been pacing the floor all morning. Go on, call him. You can take the phone into the half bath. I'll stay here and play lookout."

Maggie grins as she takes the phone around the corner into the bathroom.

While she's gone, Betty unloads the dishwasher, puts everything away, then wipes off the table and counters. Through the door she can hear the low hum of Maggie's voice, now and then the sound of laughter.

A few minutes later, Maggie emerges. She's smiling. But before Betty can say, I told you so, Maggie says, "It's for you. I was just hanging up with my certain someone when your certain someone beeped through on call waiting."

"What?"

"You know. The man with the English accent."

Betty smiles. Now it's her turn to take the phone into the half bath.

"Charlie?"

"Hello, love. I called to let you know I'm in Charlotte. Was that Jill who answered?"

"That was Maggie. Oh, Charlie. I have so much to tell you tomorrow."

"All of it good, I hope."

"You won't believe how good. You were right when you said, 'Do what you can, then let them get on with it.'"

"Sometimes that's all you can do. I . . . uh . . ." He says, sounding distracted.

"Is everything all right?"

"I hope so. I . . . uh . . . have something I need to talk to you about."

"Charlie?"

He hesitates. "I'm sorry. I shouldn't have brought it up now. It would probably be better if I told you tomorrow so we could talk face-to-face."

"You can't bring it up and not tell me. I've had enough suspense for one day."

His voice sounds strained and uncertain."You're right . . . but, I'll probably make a big hash of it . . . it's . . . uh . . . well . . . I'm thinking about selling up . . ."

"Selling up?"

"Selling my house at the beach."

She grips the receiver, but keeps her voice neutral. "Uh-huh."

"I thought I wanted the beach, but it turns out I'm not a real beach person. Maybe the odd weekend now and then, but I'm not a full-time beach person."

Oh, Lord, he's moving, Betty thinks. He was fed up with her and her problems and he's moving. He'd probably go back to England, thousands of miles away, and she'd never see him again.

"You're moving?" she says.

"I know it sounds sudden, but I've been thinking about it awhile."

Oh, no. He'd been thinking about it all these weeks while she's been tied up with her family. Now that she wants nothing more than to make him the center of her life it's too late.

"After all my son and my business are here . . . and then you . . ."

She squeezes her eyes shut and tries to concentrate on his words, but her ears are roaring. All she hears is, "my son . . . business . . . you . . ."

She sits on the toilet seat and puts her head between her knees.

"Are you still there, then, Betty."

"Still here," she mumbles.

"The thing is . . ."

"The thing is," she echoes, but her voice is faint, barely a whisper.

"I don't want to pressurize you."

"What?"

"Uh, pressure you."

"Pressure? I don't know what—"

"Oh, Betty, I knew I should have waited. I *have* made a shambles of this, but you've got to know how I feel about you."

"What did you say?"

"I've made a shambles of this?"

"I know, but what was that other thing you said?"

"It's just . . . I don't want to rush you, love . . ."

"Uh-huh."

". . . but I've decided to move back to Charlotte."

•   •   •

When Betty comes out of the bathroom, she can't seem to stop smiling, she wants to dance around the kitchen, then run out in the yard and turn cartwheels.

Maggie just looks at her. "Mother, are you all right?"

Betty laughs out loud, then crosses the room to her daughter and kisses her on the cheek.

"Mother! What in the world!" Maggie's eyes are wide, but she's smiling and sitting up straighter than she has in weeks.

Betty puts a finger to her lips, then tiptoes down the hall. A moment later she walks to the back door and looks outside. When she sees the coast is clear, she rummages under the sink, behind the trash bags and Comet and Ivory liquid until her fingers touch a dusty bottle. There it is! The homemade dandelion wine Dr. Pinckney's nurse had given her at the hospital Christmas party.

She sets the bottle on the counter, then pours a half inch into two coffee mugs and gives one to Maggie.

"Mother! When did you take up drinking?"

"This year. I had a drink last June and now this one. Let's see, that makes it two drinks this year and it's only August."

Maggie laughs. "But why are you tiptoeing around? It's not illegal and you are of age."

"Mama Dean."

"Oh, Lord. The only alcohol Mama Dean allows in the house is Eckerd rubbing alcohol," they say in unison.

They laugh again.

"I've been so cautious all my life. But I intend to celebrate today with a glass of wine. Why, I might even send out for pizza instead of cooking."

"Whoa. My own little mama's taking a walk on the wild side."

They both grin and raise their mugs. "What are we drinking to, Mother?"

"To today. To you and your girls. You and Mama Dean. You and Jerry. Oh, and did I tell you, Charlie's moving to Charlotte?"

Maggie just looks at her. "Gosh, are you all getting serious?"

Betty's heart leaps in her chest, then returns to its normal rhythm, and she understands that her life sentence of solitary confinement has ended. She looks at Maggie, and nods, calmly.

Maggie raises her mug. "Well, I guess you better marry him, then."

*Poplar Grove Exposito*r • December 14, 1985

SWEET–LOVE ENGAGEMENT ANNOUNCED

Mrs. Deanie Pruitt announces the engagement of her daughter, Elizabeth Anne Sweet, of Poplar Grove, to Charles David Love, son of the late Mr. and Mrs. Alan Love of London, England.

The bride-to-be is the daughter of the late Donley Pruitt. She is a graduate of the Raleigh School of Licensed Practical Nursing and is employed at the Poplar Grove Long Term Care Facility. The future groom is the owner of Love's Garden and Gifts and resides in Charlotte, NC.

The wedding is planned for June of 1986 at the Poplar Grove United Methodist Church.